I0686883

OH YES!
ALL MEN ARE DOGS

Other novels by the same author

My Love Never Faked...
As Long As I Love You
A Little Love Incident

As anxious readers ask: Why not another love story?
I answer: *In sitaron se agey jahan aur bhi hain,*
Abhi ishq ke imtehaan aur bhi hain...

OH YES!
ALL MEN ARE DOGS
… It's just that we have different breeds

NIKHIL MAHAJAN

Srishti
PUBLISHERS & DISTRIBUTORS

Srishti Publishers & Distributors
N-16, C. R. Park
New Delhi 110 019
editorial@srishtipublishers.com

First published by
Srishti Publishers & Distributors in 2013

Copyright © Nikhil Mahajan, 2013

Typeset by EGP at Srishti

It is not a person who is dirty,

it is the mind

[No dog was hurt in the making of this book]

Acknowledgements

Thanks to "Bade papa" for inspiring me and teaching me the meaning of "being- together." I would like to say thanks to "Destiny" to make my dreams and thoughts come true.

Again, this work cannot be complete without thanking my sweet little gf, who is always there in my mind while I write, I owe my work to her because her LOVE was special and so was the breakup. I would like to say "sorry" to her as I could not make up with her, but the promises I had made will never be broken and kept like a true gentleman.

Thanks to my pal Akhil, Amit, Prashant, Sunil and Varun who stood by my side whenever I needed them. I would also like to thank my mates "Aman" and "Jai" who traveled with me all the way from my breakup and rejections and accepting me as I am.

I would like to thank my editor who introduced me to this world of writing from where this journey became endless with his efforts and vision regarding my scripts. Thanks to all who discouraged me to write, and I wish they will keep on discouraging me in the near future because their presence is also as necessary as that of those who compliment me.

[THANKS TO PRIYANKA DEY, PRASHANT GANDHI, GAURAV CHAWLA, ILA GARG, ANKITA MAHAJAN, PUSHPENDRA HRIDEY, HITESH FOR THEIR TIMELY HELP; and sorry if I am missing any name.]

PROLOGUE

Well understanding a guy is a bit long for girls. This hum-tum ki ladai saali khatam hi nahi hoti. However, I have a very simple exegesis for this life and everything, which encircles it. I always think "All men are the same". How?

Well, all men are alike and this has been proven universally. I will explain it with an example: We; guys are like an ice cream cone; hard in nature and are the base, a protector and yet gaudy too.

Have you ever heard of different flavors of cones? Right, they are of just a few types: a simple one is just like the guys found everywhere. The other one is the chocolate flavor i.e. an athletic guy. Now the core difference between the two type is; the sporty one - the protector and the simpler one - the darling types. So these athletic guys are obstinate, non-loving and hash types. Some girls like them because of their good looks and a few for their stubborn nature whereas the simple one I mean easy in nature, loving, caring, and full time devoted types are prayerable.

However, compared to boys' girls are like an ice cream tossed into these cones. Few are dressed with jellies, some with strawberries and with other stuffings too. Different girls are meant for different cones and they fit right into them and thus make a perfect cornetto.

Always remember one thing: "All men are dogs"; I confess it today you will do it tomorrow…

How? Let's read it and find out…

1

Announcements were about to be made in an assembly in which everyone gathered. This was supposed to be a significant part of the first day of the college. Important for the teachers to introduce themselves, but dull for students who came here for studies. "Studies"; oops *sorry for using a wrong word; you people might be wondering that what I am writing.* Well we took admissions for studying Love and gathered for the practicals of our teenage mistakes.

So on the first day of BBA College, everyone gathered on the porch. But as you know, things never go the way they are supposed to. Suddenly...

"Hi babes," shouted one girl aloud waving her hand towards another girl; her friend and as an eye contact took place, they walked towards each other. They were like as if they had starved for each other for years. I wonder why girls always love to meet each other so closely, hugging each other. As they moved fast the scene virtually remained me of the one in DDLJ where Shah Rukh runs for Kajl in the yellow mustard fields and as I came back to the present scene; the girls came closer with their usual

1

hugging. As they hugged each other tightly with their tight t-shirts and perfectly fitted pants, their boobs collides with each other and they nearly popp out from their t-shirts, just the way as titanic hit an iceberg. All the men present there, watched wide eyed, their jaw wide open, and tongues drooled for more; As the two girls dog into each other's body, they looked so happy. I wondered why they never cared to meet their boyfriend with so much enthusiasm. A noticeable smile appeared on my lips. Oh God! What a panorama it was.

"Hello, roll no. 38?" said one guy who came from nowhere and offered me a hand to shake.

"Hi" I said and shook hands.

"Akash," his voice was husky and bold.

"Siddharth," I replied.

"I know," smiled Akash to me.

"How?" I inquired as it was something weird to hear on the first day of the college.

"Well just to know whose answer sheet I am going to copy from for the next three years." He explained dramatically and laughed aloud taking me into his confidence and I too laughed at his silly joke.

"I have been doing it for years." He continued sounding more confident.

"So what's up?" I started the conversation and flipping from his topic where I knew next he would be interested in telling me his stories about cheating. But more of it; it was an inquiry.

"Nothing much just looking around" he smiled at me.

"Why are these girls always ready to create a scene?" It suddenly came from my side of the conversation as I was enjoying the scene where these girls were still busy talking to each other about their pre-college shopping expenses. Here each buck spent was an act of bravery regardless of the fact that how hard it was for their parents to earn.

My concern about these girls grabbed attention of my new friend and it was a check, whether this guy was straight or not, by pointing at the two hot girls standing in the same room.

"Well this one is my girlfriend." Akash pointed out one girl of them.

"Lucky you." I smiled.

"Yes lucky for the past few years." said Akash with his collar up.

"We were course mates since I started with commerce and knew each other from coaching time. I was a commerce student with average marks. So being here and getting admission in such a prestigious institute was never my aim. I always wanted to join my father's business, but my father had something else in his mind. He was aimed to make me study and learn business tactics before I joined him." And the conversation went for a few minutes; we were on the edge of talking about his dad's turnover in the business to India's economy and corruption.

During the conversation my eyes repeatedly fell on the bombshell standing close by. I wanted to make eye contact with her she stood with Akash's girlfriend, but I could just see her well shaped behind. My curiosity increased with each second as I could not get a glimpse of her.

Suddenly, the two girls shook hands and Akash's girl friend came our way. Akash hugged his girl tight in front of me to tease me as a sign of his possessiveness. Even I would want to do the same if I had her. To be honest this girl was awesome. However, the girl who went her way after talking to Akash's girlfriend, was more mystic. I could find a connection between that girl and me and I could feel something; like on an aura from her side.

"This is Siddharth and she is my girl Jenny." said Akash to his girlfriend with a formal introduction.

"Hi" and smiles were exchanged between us.

"Oh I will introduce you to one of my old friends." she turned to call her friend and my connection.

"Piyali" she shouted and waved, but as the girl was facing another side, she could not hear her calling or her gestures. Before she could reach for her, she turned back; an announcement took place from the principal who just entered, and everybody paid attention to him standing on the stage. We hurriedly made lines as an act of obedience, but I was still disturbed about this girl whom I could not see. I again tried to look her side to get a glimpse but could not, as the room was overcrowded. Standing in the line, I made endless attempts but failed each time. Then as one of the teachers took hold of the mike, it was a perfect chance for me to change my place. I went to have a look at her, but suddenly she turned other side and so did I simultaneously. I was again on the wrong side, and one more attempt failed. I wondered why I was so curious about her and it was quite obvious for Jenny to notice. For me, it was like now or never.

"Are you comfortable?" Akash inquired.

"Yeah," I replied still looking for this girl on the one side and not concentrating on the speech being delivered.

Finally, with the note of thank and a call for the class, the teacher took us to a class for our first curriculum lecture. We obeyed and followed her like herd of sheep. While we entered our new class it was the perfect time for me to make my last attempt to have a glance of this beautiful girl. I ran breaking the line towards her. I touched her shoulder...

"What?" said Jenny to me as she walked along with this girl who was now a part of her gang. I was pretty sure that this girl would also stop as her friend, but she walked away.

"What happen to her?" I asked Jenny.

"What?"

"I wanna see this girl" I went straight.

"Piyali," uttered Jenny confused. Jenny shouted her name loudly. With the call, she turned back... and I was surprised...

"Leave her; I am not interested to talk to her." I walked away.

"Why?" Jenny came to me hitting me with her question.

"I am not going to class; if you are interested let's move to the canteen." I looked disturbed, which was easily perceptible on my face.

"Are you okay?" Jenny wanted to know.

"Yeah" I was sweating now.

"Yeah let's move; let me have water." Jenny took hold of my hand as I felt like collapsing.

"Akash, to the canteen..." she called her boyfriend to help her to hold me and we all went to the canteen. Jenny tried inviting Piyali; her new gang member but Piyali went to the class which was rather rude.

Before we move further into the story let's get introduced. I am Siddharth you can say the Dog no. 1, adding to the list Akash was the Dog no. 2. Well there were so many dogs around but we knew only a few. This was my 1st day at BBA College based in Delhi. Life for me was never firmer; my father was a businessman, and I did not at any time cared much about money. Akash's father was in the Indian embassy. I still wonder why I never found him pleased with his dad and neither Akash's father Mr. Sharma, nor was her mother happy with him. However, it has nothing to do it with me and the story. Jenny was Akash's girl friend; one of the most beautiful girls around but she was already hooked with my friend; else I don't know since when they knew each other, but everyone said they were lovers since they had been in their diapers. What a fuck it was; but it was true.

@
2nd day of the college

It was a boring day and to get used to the new people around and to the fresh schedule, we decided to throw a party. Delhi is the capital not only for this country's business hubs but also a capital of parties and pubs.

In the midst of a boring class suddenly my mobile beeped. There was a message and I clicked to read it without wasting anytime.

"So the party in the Ashe Lounge." I read the text.

"No I don't know?" I texted back.

"Everyone is attending." a reply came.

"Is Piyali included in everyone; here?" I texted back to confirm.

"No." Akash texted back.

"Then I will join you." and I looked at him sitting near to Piyali in her group, we exchanged smiles for the conformation but Akash was a little confused because just a day back I was dying to meet this girl and now I was ignoring her.

Few hours later in the canteen...

"What if she also joins us?" said Akash to me in front of Jenny while he put down his cold drink on the table after taking a sip. Jenny took this same drink and she sipped from the same straw. I wonder why lovers always share cold drinks and the straw.

"I am not going then." I replied while putting both my hands on the table, and a stance that I was ending this dialogue with a straight answer.

"C'mon this is bullshit." said Jenny to me offering me, the same cold drink which I refused and she returned it to Akash.

"Are you silly; we arranged this party so that you could get introduced to this girl; Akash told me you were interested, and you have asked him about this girl on the first day.? So don't be a spoil sport. Just be a man, don't be shy just give a try..." she continued endlessly trying to motivate me.

"Nothing from my side." I replied.

"Then let's cancel this trip" said Jenny to me taking the bottle in her hand from

Akash angrily, though there was hardly any sip left in it.

"Can you please stop sharing this same cold drink bottle? C'mon use two straws at least **yaar**…" I walked away taunting them.

"This guy seriously has some problem with Piyali. Ask him Akash, she is in my group and my friend. I have known her for the last two years." I could hear the comments from Jenny as I walked out from the canteen but who cares what they said behind my back.

That evening a text came from Jenny about the cancellation of the plan to which I texted "Sorry" to her and then no message was exchanged then after.

Next day in the college again…

As I opened the door, I did not notice Piyali coming from the other side. I was not sure she was about to enter the room. The handle was in my hand, and the one hurt badly was Piyali. As her hand touched the door hard she screamed, more loudly than the door hit her hand. I knew it was just drama.

"Fuck you." Piyali screamed aloud at me without thinking anything and the situation.

"That's what you deserve." I replied back; I knew she was hurt but I reacted in the same way exposing us both to the trouble.

"You are a dog." Piyali cried aloud in front of the whole class.

"Not you, all men are dogs." she continued, and she looked towards Akash this time complimenting him too along with me.

"You mind your language lady; I am not even talking to you." I looked at her in anger.

I pushed her hard in front of everyone making a way for myself. As I walked inside with the bag in my hand, my bag again hit her throwing her on the door and this time it was done intentionally. I took the last seat in no time without looking at her.

"What a loser!" She too came in holding her injured hand trying to attain sympathy from the whole class.

However, everyone was stunned at the incident and our reactions. It was the beginning as a storm was brewing.

"I wonder what these guys think of themselves?" She screamed aloud looking at the whole last row of boys increasing her inclusion criteria of her allegations.

"Jay-Sean." One guy said aloud.

"Huh!" another rebellious girl moaned in class from the first row.

"Get lost whosoever has a problem here" one guy from the last row took the guys, side.

And before the fight could develop into a ***hum tum*** thing the teacher entered the class and the big fight ended.

A few hours later Piyali struck me again but this time the volcano was red hot near the water cooler. Before I could say or do anything…

"I wanna drink water and you just pushed me," said Piyali to me before I could grab the glass.

"Huh!" I showed her the tap which was under my control now.

"C'mon why the hell will I push you? Get aside." as I tried hard to save my situation.

"Fuck you." She pushed me with her shoulder and hold on to the tap.

"What was that?" I looked at her as she smiled back.

"Hey I am warning you, you dare not come my way, or else I will screw you." I tried to scare her this time.

"I am not interested." She filled her glass and drank water. With the last big gulp, she dropped the glass on the floor. I knew it was going to happen. She knew I needed this so I saved myself with an attempt to drink water with my hands.

As I bent down to drink water, I felt water just flowing down over my back. **Oh my God,** the girl had almost puked water filled in her mouth; the one last sip had been just to spit it out on my shirt.

I shouted aloud "Bitch bitch…" with my **middle finger salute**.

"Loser, well I will spell it for you." She smiled again with the same energy and walked towards the stairs as she knew I would follow her in revenge.

"L - O - S - E - R" she repeated aloud which makes me angrier.

"And fuck you" she said aloud with such vengeance that everyone around looked at us fighting. I ran toward's her and she ran towards the class. The class was upstairs so we both tried our best. She ran fast and entered the class and I ran hard to catch her before she could reach her destination.

In anger I opened the door of the class with a blow; I looked at all the rows to get a view of her standing at the end. I had entered the room for the revenge, and my hard hit on the door was audible to the teacher who was inside.

The clock ticked here steadily as I little by little turned towards the teacher, and the teacher gaped upon me and said something which I could not understand. My ears were red hot; I came to my senses and found myself in trouble. I tried to read the teacher's lips to find what he was saying to me.

I concentrated more. I could hear only one-word… as I came to reality…

"Out" shouted the Professor.

"What sir… I mean," I stammered, all confused.

"Out I say" he repeated in anger.

"Sir…" I tried to explain.

I was wrong I tried not to be bullied by him. I went outside the class, while I could hear everyone laughing at me. I was the new super hero of the class, the first rule breaker.

I again did a middle finger salute to Piyali, but to my bad luck suddenly Professor turned and saw me. With his eyebrow raised thinking I was saluting him…

"Come what you want to say with that finger I will make you do," said the Professor.

"Sorry sir." I tried to show some shame and looked at the floor this time helpless.

Within seconds I counted the number of tiles on the floor, keeping myself busy while he was busy yelling at me.

"No." The Professor's anger was not going to cool down I knew it well.

"Sir" I stammered again but this time at the thought that my father will be called upon.

"Out for 5 days."

"Thank you oops! Sorry Sir." I was confused whether to be happy or feel sad.

"20 days out and call your father." the Professor was more strict than I had thought. I kept mum so as not to make any more mistakes.

Few hours later at ground

My luck was pushed to the limits and this bad luck was not ending ever since I had met Piyali. So much bad luck in a single day, it had never happened to me.

"This boy is cute but there is some problem with him." Said one of the girl signaling at me, while Piyali was talking to her about something; I guess about me.

"He's a psycho." Piyali said.

I tried to ignore so as not to cause any more nuisance.

"C'mon Piyali why do you think so?" Said the girl, again taking my side.

"He is, you know **HANDSOME** kind of guy; he is…," said Piyali aloud so that I should hear it.

As soon as I heard **HANDSOME**, I could not hold my anger, and I came for a fight.

"Hey whom you're calling it loser?" said I to her, words she just uttered to me.

"Mind your business." I continued.

However, the girl was not about to hold herself, and I could not to scare her. Akash saw me with Piyali, and he knew we were fighting. He ran towards me to hold me. As he held me from the back and tried taking me aside I threw his hand.

"Akash tell her not to talk to me or about me." I shouted adding to the mess.

"Even I am not interested" She retorted loudly, adding a few more words to her angry reaction and her loud presence.

"Loser." she continued.

"That's what you can do." she kept on uttering harsher words as Akash took me to the other side of the ground, but our eye contact did not break.

"Hey you stay here man. Why are you people fighting and what's this? You were about to hit a girl. Where are your manners?"

"Okie, I am relaxed." I tried to apologize.

"Think." Jenny came to my side.

"Why do you when an idiot when you see Piyali?" She questioned.

"What?" said I; looking straight into her eyes.

"Nothing chill. We are going clubbing now. Dare you to say no to me." She tried to flirt with me in front of Akash.

"Whatever." I said as I left the ground while Piyali was already out with her two other friends.

"But Piyali is cute." said Akash to me.

"I thought you peeked into her on the first day as she met Jenny."

"Those were other times when I didn't know she was Piyali."

"What's wrong with Piyali?"

"Piyali herself is wrong." I barked.

"And now, please stop this conversation." I said as I grabbed my bag, and we left the school after a hectic day and a big fight.

2

In Café Lounge

As I inhaled my first puff of nicotine; from the hookahs` pipe which was placed in front of us on the table. Akash took hold of the pipe for his turn and passed it to Jenny.

"So what?" asked Akash to Jenny, as a streak of smoke comes out from her nostrils with the nose-ring, sparkling. Her dress sense, spilling black lipstick on her lips and the nail paint made her a slutty *emo-girl.*

"Nothing." I looked for my chance to take a puff.

"You still not over her and deep into your head you are making plan for revenge." Jenny bent down showing her deep cleavage. She knew they were so huge and noticeable. "Fuck her."

"You have some problem with her?" asked Jenny while handing me the mouth piece of the hookah after another round.

"You are looking handsome." said Jenny to Akash.

"Really!" Akash kissed on her lips and a lip-lock happened next.

"***Naah*** Handsome is an informal compliment" I said looking at the way Jenny put her tongue in Akash's mouth, and he sucked it hard. Her tongue rolled in his mouth just like a fish kept on the hot pan. Steaming and shaking.

"Did she say something worng?" the lip lock broke and the two highly flushed lusty love birds looked at me.

"Piyali called you handsome on the college campus and it doesn't mean it changes the meaning of this word in the dictionary." said Jenny laughing at me, while Akash was still busy with the hookah.

Lemme explain to you; "I think it needs a little elaboration here…" and very dramatically I started.

"If sex with three people is called a threesome, and sex with two people is called a twosome, now can you understand why they call someone handsome?"

"Do I look like that?" I questioned.

"I got my friend back on track." Akash patted my back and suddenly everyone almost laughed aloud and the tension in the atmosphere dissolved and the anger so volatile in nature just vanished.

Next morning at the college

The teacher came to the class and made an announcement about our first project. It was a poster presentation competition which we all ought to participate to show our commanding skills.

"Are you people going to make your groups yourself, or do I have to interfere and make them for you?" said the teacher looking at the class which was looking disinterested as nobody was prepared to study so early in the academies session. No one replied and it was clear we required assistance.

"Okay I will do it myself." she said.

And the announcements were made in the class regarding the group formation three boys and one girl in each group.

"The remaining ones please come this side. I will group you together." said the teacher as she grouped the good students of the class in the first few groups and remaining ones were left to each other's mercy.

My name was not announced and it was clear I was considered mediocre. So I went to the other side. But I was happy to see Jenny and Akash joining me too. Suddenly I found myself standing along with Piyali. I stepped back and moved to one of the finest groups in the class. My motive was to keep myself away from her; I stood there but my teacher happened to notice me standing at the wrong place.

"What are you doing there Siddharth?" she looked at me and asked for a clarification.

"Come to this side we will make your group with this girl." she pointed at me. Then she pointed towards Piyali the one I hated most and signaled to me to stand along with her. I was helpless. I could not say anything, but I knew what I had to do. Finally another disastrous decision was made unintentionally, and I was grouped along with Piyali. I nodded, and we started with the title of the poster preparation. I took the most important part of the competition - the presentation.

Finally, none of us neither Piyali nor I attended the poster presentation and discussion part, thinking we might face each other that way. On the final day competition my absence from the presentation confirmed that this fight was taking a bad shape. We lost our first assignment, and everyone in the group got zero because of me for which Piyali insulted me in front of the whole class.

I was sad for the other students in the group. Because of me; their marks also went down. So to cheer me up, Jenny and Akash insisted that I join them in a booze party that night to which I could not resist.

In the party

I was in the club and on the main service table. Drinks were served, and spirits were high. However, as usual Jenny and Akash hit me with the same lame questions.

"Dude seriously you failed in the first academic performance, and you are partying for it all because you wanted to see Piyali failing. What a shame!."

"Man what kind of mother fucker shit is this?" Akash smiled.

"Hatred has its rule but you followed none, and this is bad I must say." He continued.

"I don't like it when I ask you something, and you look at the other way.

Look into my eyes there is something you are hiding."

"Rules?" I replied back.

"Yes rules man, had you ever heard about them?"

"Then I must say nobody follows rules here." I gave my explanation for my dirty political mind game.

"What kind of thing are saying you?"

"You know what Love guru says: It is very tough once the toothpaste is out of the tube and the same is with relationships; once you are out you are out." I gave him an example.

"Fuck your love guru and this tooth paste example" Akash replied irritated.

"Dare you disrespect Love guru?" I warned.

"Okay sorry but you have to tell us the scene behind the scene. Who knows we might also start hating Piyali too if your clarification is fair enough. Or is it that you failed a little girl just because of your ego."

"Ego? No man this is revenge!"

"What kinda revenge?" Akash and Jenny were confused this time.

"You know what? She was my girlfriend long back when I was in 8th standard"

"What????" said Akash and Jenny together.

3

+++*Love guru says: We never care about what's on our side of the table; it's always about what's on the other side.* +++

"Hey! Tell me about your love story man; how you proposed to her?" asked Akash.

"What happened between the two of you that it turned so bad? How did this love turn into hatred? Look it is common that relationship ends either in a good way or in a silence, but your case seems to be different," he continued in curiosity.

"Leave it **yaar** I don't want to discuss it." I tried changing the topic.

"What?" he asked again.

"Nothing" I replied.

+++ *Wise men say: Fuck your past.... Just don't let it fuck you....* +++

"C'mon you have to tell us if you think we are your best friend." This time it was a very specific statement.

As I heard the word FRIEND it took me to the past and I started narrating my love life to of them.

"You tricked me." I started narrating dramatically.

Finally the brutal love Confession

To get something you've never had, you must be willing to do something you've never done.

My life was easy because it was without girls. It happened when I was in the 8th standard. We were five friends in groups – all boys. In our group, girls were not allowed until one-day Kunal saw some weird movie in an English channel. New to the life encounters, he narrated the whole story to us. It was a 15+ movie under parental guidance. He was pretty sure about a girlfriend thing. But no one agreed. However, everyone in their heart's heart started searching for that lucky girl. We were all kids. I was the one who was the shortest of all.

On one morning at the prayer time in school, I saw my angel; she stood next to me; in front, in the girl row. I could not believe my fate; she just matched my height. I was astonished by her beauty; I had never noticed her in class. That day I decided that I would have her as my girlfriend. And then the problem started.

"Hey I thought a lot about the girlfriend thing, and then I decided I should have a girlfriend, what say?" I confessed with a heavy heart of being rejected.

"What you are talking about?" Questioned one of the friends from my group.

"A girl in the group," I revealed.

"Yeah," I smiled and waited for an appropriate answer.

"But…" Everyone was confused by my sudden confession.

"It's okay," replied Kunal to dilute the tension in the group.

"I too want to confess that I am in love," he continued.

"Who?" Everyone looked at him with their eyes opened as he rivaled the secret.

"Piyali."

"Oh shit man, she is mine," uttered one of the other members of our gang as he looked unhappy.

Thus it was revealed that at the same time all of my friends were infatuated with the girl. We were all smitten by the same girl. Then we decided that we would propose to her together. Knowing nothing about what we were doing we proposed to her.

"What happened then?" Asked Jenny to me as she entered the room.

"I heard about you and Piyali being together in-school days."

"Hm…" I could say only this much.

"And now?" She asked.

"Nothing now." I took a deep breath.

"No hard feelings." I continued.

"No. I am asking about the soft feelings," she tried to peel me.

"So what happened? Piyali agreed to your proposal and rejected every one else?" Akash was more interested about the love story.

"Nope." I answered.

"Then?" he asked in curiosity.

"She agreed." I said to Jenny and Akash with an angelic smile.

THE PROPOSAL

"You mean you all?" Said Piyali looking at us. We were all gelled with well combed hair, stood in front of her looking like idiots.

"Yes" said Kunal looking into her.

"All?" Piyali laughed.

"Yes." I interfered this time, and I smiled.

It was teen age, and we were too innocent to realize what we were doing. Having a girlfriend, was a prestige issue rather than having her as one.

"But still, why me?" Piyali was way smart to think what was in our mind, but still she played with her words.

"Because none of us matched to the height, we all are short for other girls in the class, so we decided to make you our girl friend."

To our joint venture for this girlfriend thing Piyali reacted in a very wise way.

"You know what the meaning of a girlfriend is?" questioned Piyali.

"It means good friend." I tried to justify.

"Best friend as they say." I continued.

"And what else?"

"They kiss sometimes." Kunal added to the answer to give more justification and clarification.

"You mean I should kiss all of them?" She pointed towards everyone standing there in a saw.

"If you wish to." I was running out of answers now and my heart was pounding too.

"Nope I won't be doing that." Piyali refused.

"But first let's go for the maintenance charges." She now put down her proposal.

"What's that?" Kunal questioned.

"That means I need to be maintained for you people; you have to gift me something."

"Better if you pay me half of your pocket money," she seeded smart.

"You mean half of it?" Kunal confirmed.

"If I am your partner, I mean I am now, it means I am half of your life investment, isn't it?" She gave a clever excuse to hide her greediness.

"So half of your pocket money should be mine."

"Or you can pay installments." She gave another option.

"How much do you get each day?" She was now acting like our official girlfriend sucking our blood.

"50 rupees." Kunal answered

"Then pay me 25 bucks out of it."

"And you Sid you have to pay me 35 bucks." I was gunshot this time.

"Why?" I asked.

"Because I don't like your face." and it was a sudden unexpected insult.

I had no choice but to accept her because it was a question of my reputation now. I agreed. Nothing good happened later as my life turned into hell and so did my reputation; subsequently it happened as…

A KISS NEVER TO BE MISSED

Being a boyfriend and never being kissed was something not soothing but Piyali was single having four idiots around her. To kiss everyone was a difficult job for her. It could never go smoothly until Piyali came with a thought from the TAMBOLA game. It was a lottery and a pure chance where everyone's luck will help to touch those pink lips.

To my bad luck, I could never reach them. It was always Kunal who kissed her. And then I decided to rip every friend apart to make her mine and for this I started with tricks. *It's funny how you think you are playing someone, when in all reality you are the one being played.* A bad reputation is an easy trick. So I decided to strike and rip my friends with it.

Trick 1
Sex is a noun not verb

On a very good day of mine a bad day for my friend I started with my first elimination.

"She's wearing pink panties."

"And the one are you looking at on your right has white panties." I continued courting him.

"What the mother fucker is this and how you know the color?" my friend was excited.

"Hey I have a trick for it."

"What trick?" he asked.

"Ok lemme tell you this trick as you insist so much."

"You just stand here near the stairs and when someone will go up or down; just peep up you will be able to see what you wished to." I smiled.; I knew he was tricked. He was the easiest one to trap.

"What?" he questioned idiotically.

"USA."

"What USA?"

"U – under, S – Skirt, A – Area." I explained.

"Heaven." I continued to impress him with my IQ and self made abbreviations.

"And you will definitely feel Japan."

"What Japan?"

"J- Jumping, A- and, P – Pumping, A- all, N- night." I explained more moving my hand up and down.

"Fuck you man lemme try this."

And this was what I wanted to. Mission accomplished now the second part of the real trick, I called upon the vice captain of the school told her the whole story about the skirt thing and blamed it on my friend. I became innocent. Captain of the school was furious as she caught him watching panties and grabing color, at the foot of the stairs. He got screwed up and I went to Piyali straight away just striking him out of her list. Now there were three left in the Piyali court who shares her as a girlfriend.

Trick 2
If I don't like it then you too have to dislike it.

I was just wondering how to trick my second friend and then I had an Idea. I searched for a roach and put it into a matchbox. I took that match box into the tuition class. That day I didn't sit next to Piyali as we were all fighting for her. I opened the match box and threw it towards Piyali slowly without her noticing it. I could see the roach proceeding toward her but suddenly my friend noticed it and as he was never scared of it he just picked it up with its aniline. It was a sudden threat to my plan.

"Hey Piyali watch out." I cried aloud to grab her attention.

"What?"

She screamed aloud as she saw him holding the roach in his hand and helplessly sitting in the middle of the room he could not do anything than throwing it and somehow it fell on Piyali.

Mission accomplished. I knew girls were always scared of lizards and roach and I would have arranged for a lizard that day but could not manage one.

But now we were two who were with Piyali. I was the one she never liked and the second one was Kunal whom she loved desperately. To trick him was a real buster and none of my ideas could help me here.

That day something happened, which should never have. I noticed Piyali and Kunal tricking me with the Tambola game. It was known to all of us that Piyali liked him more than anyone else and always used to take him for consideration. Now it was I who was going to fuck him hard.

Trick 3
To break trust is an easy way to break a relationship.

I knew I could never reach Piyali's lips so on a very fine day I decided to meet her near the chemistry lab. It was the place where the mystery was going to take place. I begged Piyali for the first kiss of my lifetime and this was where it happened. I begged her a lot for it. I fell to her feet for those pink lips. For a few minutes of begging finally Piyali got convinced about the kiss but just a tender touch and nothing much. As it happened my messenger called Kunal to come and see.

Finally Kunal saw what he never intended to. As my love guru says: *To know something which need not to be known is more hurting than to know it, intentionally or unintentionally.* Piyali broke Kunal's trust and the relationship too and was only mine now. But destiny had something else for us.

We were not the only love birds in the school. Piyali was somehow involved with some eleventh standard student because he could give her a ride on his bike from school to her neighborhood. It was now known that to fight with this guy was tough.

+++ *Destiny as defined by wise men: I'd rather have a fucked up truth, than a believable lie.* +++

But I was depressed and wanted Piyali to have a break up with this guy before she left me. *As my love guru says: Sacrifices are always made for some good reason.*

I sacrificed my morals that day for my love. I started a fight with Piyali's new boyfriend and let his brother know about him. His brother called me up and our group of friends lied about our status. We made up a story about how Piyali had been involved with this guy. We never looked for the after effects of our story but it took a bad shape and Piyali left the school afterward leaving our heart and lips missing her.

"And now as we find ourselves landing in the same college"

"This hatred has turned into revenge." I continued narrating the story to Jenny and Akash.

"Awesome man." Akash freaked out.

"Interesting." Said Jenny with a half smile on her face. I always wondered what this half smile meant – *an expression of sympathy or disdain.*

4

There is a simple equation in Mathematics where you have to make LHS equal to RHS to solve the problem (right-hand side = left-hand side; if you remember).

In sex too we have the same equation, a bf and sex are like LHS equals to RHS. Wonder how?

Let solve this equation before to move further…

First LHS means "let's have sex", and RHS is "right to have sex". So what make them equal here is *"A boyfriend has all the right to fuck his girl friend as his fundamental right so let's have sex here means he owe to have sex, with all laws of love and sex."*

Summer 1st year; BBA and heedless I was given the next project with Piyali by the class representative with a machination from Akash and Jenny. I had no option other then join her in this project; else the reputation which was now left after what I did to the rest of the classmates during my poster presentation competition may drown.

I never expected anything like this from Jenny Akash I knew I had no way out as I fucked-up everyone in the Poster presentation, so I gave up the regular blame game. This time my strategy was way different. I decided to give a try with Piyali rather than a fight.

And even Piyali's side was also soft. So we wisely chose our topic on "Indian Entrepreneur," it was a mutual decision. Working together on our project and downloading few power points from Google over the topic in Piyali's room; Jenny and Akash too joined us for help.

Suddenly, to distract our hectic schedule, Jenny told us the story of a Hollywood movie she watched last night "Hangover." We all freaked out hearing the story and decided to watch it together in Piyali's room on her laptop. Piyali gave us a blanket as it was raining outside and cold too.

We wrapped ourselves in the blanket, and Jenny made some space next to Akash as she wanted him to sit near her. I tried sitting next to Akash, but they had some personal under blanket activities which I could interrupt; so I hung up with Piyali and sat next to her.

And we all started watching the movie and on Jenny's request, Akash turned the light dim. Jenny and Akash started the movie and they came real close hugging each other. I was still struggling with Piyali as she was a real rival for me.

But as wise men says *"She has the tendency to melt you with the heat she has in her body, all you need is a tender touch to destroy yourself"*; now my hands were touching Piyali's hand, and I felt a connection from my side. To find her reaction, I looked into Piyali's eyes, they looked beautiful as always. I could see myself drowning in them long before in my childhood, today was just a realization. I was in love with her when she used to play double games with me. I could never swallow the insult I had the last time when she left me but now the moment was romantic, I touched her hand to which she did not respond. I knew there was something cooking on her side too. She looked at me; I tried not to look at her this time and try to escape the eye contact. I was all set to fire, but I kept looking at the Laptop screen, but now I could not understand even a single dialogue. My senses were occupied with her presence in my mind.

I again touched her hand, and she responded to it too gracefully. As I kept my hand on her hand, she with her other hand covers the contact with the blanket. I was all filled with the desires. I try to go for a bold move now. I slid my hand in her t-shirt. Piyali took her little tweety toy towards herself covering my hand and place it to cover my hand's presence in her top. It was a perfect response I was expecting. I now reached her bra. I tried touching her bra cups. They were perfect to feel. I could feel the shape and size of her breasts. The texture of her bra was light, and thus I could feel her hard nipples in them. They became harder as I press them hard from outside. She gazed at me silently with her lusty eyes as if she was enjoying it. I again pricked her tits with my finger tenderly and not harming them. This time she pressed her Tweety toy hard to her breasts, pressing my hand. It was just wonderful and now I proceed further. I lifted her bra; with her consent and a little effort, I manage to remove one cup of her bra. Now her one breast was out and was ready to be fondled. For the next two hours, I kept playing with her boob, and she just moaned a little in response. I could feel her nipple's areola, which was also good to enjoy. I could now feel her urge with the little breaths and shaking tummy. And many a times she looked at me with a wishful sight, but I kept concentrating on my duty of fulfilling her lust and my volcano in my pants.

The movie was over, and she pressed down my hand and poked it all-out of her shirt. She looked at me showing a little anger in her eyes. I too kept my hand at its places like a true gentleman. Suddenly, Jenny jumped towards the switch and pressed it lightening the room, and everything went to normal like before.

However, in our heart, I Piyali and I knew something had gone much further, and it could never come back to usual now. Piyali went to the kitchen for the tea, and I followed her leaving the other couple in the bedroom for privacy; rather finding privacy for myself too.

Piyali was busy preparing tea. I suddenly came from the back and press her hard with my volcano touching the buttock showing my man hood and this is how dogs as well as other animals prepare their partner. That day I realized man is a social animal. Piyali responded bending her head down.

"What was that?" I asked.

"Nothing." The reply came.

"What's there in the room which is not here?" I questioned.

She did not say anything. I tried to lighten the moment this time. I came close. Piyali got scared. I was closer to scare her and so close that I could feel her breath, and our lips were just close to each other.

"Stop it Sid." Piyali's breathing were heavy this time, and she was losing control.

"Stop what?" I asked.

"Nothing," she again changed the topic.

"Let's end it here." she continued.

"No, it was not finished, not at any time Piyali, never..." I moaned and was almost crying at this point of time.

I tried to scare her again and abruptly my lips touched her lips, and we went from a joke to kissing. Suddenly, she realized she was kissing her enemy. She threw me out with her hand on my chest and pushes me aside.

"What?" I asked confused.

"Please don't kiss." she requested.

"Why?"

"Don't." she requested again.

I again kissed her on her neck forcefully this time, and she put the knife on my neck as her reaction.

"I swear I will kill you." she warned.

I kissed her again, and she threw the knife. Suddenly, she stopped and requested. "Let's stop it here, please."

"Huh, I was not going to stop now."

"Can you give me a valid reason when you are responding to my kiss then why can't we end this fight here and...?" I kept kissing while talking.

"Look there is a reason."

"What reason?"

"If you kiss me on my neck, it's done. We're fucking." She said

"Let's fuck then." I gave her the best option.

+++ As wise men say: SEX is like snow, you never know how many inches you're going to get or how long it's going to last! +++

I smiled and suddenly Piyali smiled back too. Actually, we both wanted this to happen. I closed the door quickly, and Piyali took off her t-shirt and raised her skirt. I put my hand on her waist and pushed her hard to the wall. I then turned her while kissing over the shelves and raised her and made her sit on them. I unzipped my pants and opened it; throwing it down. Piyali put her hand in my underwear and pushed it down with my assets thrown over her. Both of us knew the time was short. So I entered her without foreplay.

After 5 minutes, we were over and tea was ready to be served. We were dressed up again. And the combined studies kept regularly. As love Guru says: *Treat her like a Queen. Fuck her like a Slut. Trust me never do that because I did it and then she start calling me Dog one day.*

THE DOGGY POSE

One day after perfect sex together hotness shed on the bed, I felt like peeing. I could not control myself. This was something I never wanted to do. I had to rush to her bathroom.

There are three rules of a girl's bathroom:

1. Everything is finely placed.
2. Commode seat is nicely cleaned and if a guy will pee standing will definitely soil it.

3. The pee style is not a free style of a man.

I was in the situation where I could not stand and pee. I was helpless to soil the seat and to perform a freestyle standing so to my rescue. I saw the wash basin shining like a pearl, and it was ready for my rescue. I got the idea and it was to pee into it. I raise one of my legs to reach the hole of the basin and opened my pants. I slid my hot rod near it and release the pressure. I was relieved and lay my head on the mirror, and suddenly I say Piyali entering the bathroom. I could not do anything as I was still emptying my bladder.

"What the fuck are you doing?" she screamed.

"What?" I replied back.

"You are trying to fuck my basin," and that was sillier I expected.

"No… No darling you are getting me wrong." I explained.

"Am I not good enough for you?" she asked.

"Oh I was not fucking the basin."

"What the hell you were doing there in the basin raising your leg like a dog?" she screamed again without hearing anything from my side.

"Oh God I was looking like a dog I agree, but I was trying to clean myself up." I tried to explain.

"You know it is good to clean yourself." I continued.

"Come-on be a support to something you are doing well as you always say I don't keep my things clean."

"You have problems with my stinking socks too!" I exclaimed more explanations.

"And my hair cut too, and now I am cleaning myself after a shag, you are pointing at me." Everything was silent for a moment; I knew I had rescued myself.

"I am sorry I thought you were masturbating after sex with me."

"It is okay." I replied.

Anyhow she did not come to know that I was actually peeing there and I changed the topic.

Over the phone

Sex was now a regular practice.

Rings

"Hello." Piyali said from the other side.

"Hi." I replied.

"I was missing you." She went straight to the topic.

"Missing me?" I wondered.

"Yes, yesterday it was awesome; I can still feel pain there." She started flirting with me.

I laughed.

"C'mon, you got a monster down there." She just talked about my size and I could not resist flirting her.

"Wise men call it the: *power of sex.*" I laughed.

"And you got volcanoes." I was witty with her.

"Shut up and close your eyes." I continued, I knew the heat she had stored for me.

"Are your eyes are closed?" I asked.

"Yes" She replied.

"I knew"

"How do you know that?" she questioned.

"I know it." I smiled.

"Okie let me tell you what am wearing." she said again to cross check.

"I know what you are wearing." my answer made the conversation more interesting.

"Then answer me." she was confused.

"Bra and panty" I laughed aloud after my silly joke to which she also responded the same way.

The scene became more intense and we played with words. She fingered herself and I shook my tool imagining each other and finally shedding myself.

"Did you come?" I asked.

"No."

"You left me thirsty." she was all wet and lusted.

"You have your other phone?"

"Yeah."

"Let me call on it with my landline, use it as a vibrator."

Then I rang her on her phone several times till she moaned hard and came gushing. It was something new but enjoyable as it was phone over the sex, so safe.

Sex was a major knot between us. We were together and enjoying ourselves. And we happened to call each other on two to three days to seduce and have phone sex. It was safe and started happening very often now.

But things between me and Piyali could not remain good for much time. Both of us had the devil in our minds. I recorded her moans over my phone and spread it between my friends and the good option ended with a fight.

SHE ADMITTED SHE LIKED IT

+++ *As love guru says: India is not a free sex country but sex is everywhere, whenever Indians get time and chance... Well do we have sex before or after the pizza comes? No matter who cares we whether have both Pizzas with sauce and of course Sex*+++

Finally the confession: Finally, the end of the fight which was somewhat fortuitous; I confessed all my deeds, and Piyali too confronted herself for her mean behaviors. I confessed my tricks, which were, to a degree, my mistakes to which Piyali could not react more than laughing out loud. Whatever happened in the past was now forgotten and a new life with sprouts of friendship with benefits of sex was served hot to us.

We had one more sex encounter which was again adventurous where we played with the ice.

In the room, after the sex "Can I have this bra of yours as a token of love?"

"What will you do with it?" Piyali replied unhooking it again.

"Just as a token."

"Only if I will have something in return from your side?" I looked at her stunn.

"What do you want?" I questioned.

"A love bite."

"…on my breast." She whispered in my ear and then licks it inserting her tongue in it giving me a shiver and my dick went hard.

"Which one is your favorite?" I pointed at the two melons in front of me.

"The right one." she gave a witty smile.

"Right is always right and leave the left." She smiled and gave me her right breast to chew.

I opened my mouth and put her breast fully into my mouth and suck it hard to harden her nipples. Her nipple went hard. I could see the stiffness even in the areola.

I then again spread my teeth over her breasts and try to bite it. I gave a little clench not hurting her; she stiffened her body with pain and a moan. I then with my hand tried to see whether the bite was successful or not. It was still an unsuccessful thing.

I tried again. This time with more pressure in my clench, I bit a little skin of her breast to give her a love bite, but no success as I looked at the bite.

"What happened Sid?" she asked.

"I am unable to." I said.

"Try again this time look at my face when you bite." She moans along with it.

I concentrated more on her face than my bite and her facial expression let me take the decision that how much was how useful. I bit her hard till she bit her lips and then I released leaving a mark.

"Thank you." she looked at the bite.

"Can I have this bra now please?" I asked.

"You won it, it's all yours." she threw the bra at my face as a gift.

I smiled back.

5

NO GLOVE NO LOVE POLICY

"I think I am pregnant." I was head to heal in sweat after hearing it that we had un-safe sex and I was a father in the middle of my student life.

"Oh! Fuck, say you not are serious?" I asked to confirm.

"I am serious." Piyali replied again.

"You didn't use protection." I continued our blame game.

"You knew where we could have stopped but…" I tried to rescue myself.

"It happened that day itself and many a times I never used but I thought you must be using pills." I shielded myself.

"But now I am pregnant." she cried.

"Is it a confession or I am told to be taking the charge of this baby now?" I asked.

"It's not late we can consult a gynecologist." I suggested.

"No I want this baby of ours." Piyali being silly.

43

"C'mon meet me in an hour we have to solve it, who else knew about this?" I questioned.

"Jenny and Akash" she replied.

"You means everybody knew it and only the father was the one left to be told" I was trembling but I tried holding myself because at this pint of time I had to stand with Piyali.

"Meet me in an hour near GK-2." I ordered her life a husband.

"Okay."

And I immediately wasting no time drop a message to Akash to meet us at the decided place.

GK-2

As my auto rickshaw stopped at GK-2 mall I in no time ran inside the parking lot. I saw Piyali standing there under the sun.

"Hey you are carrying a baby in your womb and silly girl can't you find a shady place to stand?" I said in anger looking at her.

I then covered her head with my hand to protect her from sun.

"Come this way." I held her hand.

"I was just waiting here so that you could find me easily." she replied.

"Come have some water you should not dehydrate yourself."

"Congrats" Piyali looked into my eyes. My fear was gone I was feeling like a father.

I always hated kids but today when it was all about my child I felt myself complete. I had never felt like this before. I could imagine myself carrying a small baby in my hand.

I imagined the baby there and then...

A baby girl; whose eyes like me, hair like Piyali, nose like me, lips like her, ear like me, neck like her.

"Sidi" Piyali distracted me.

"Yeah" I asked

"What? She looked at me and I shrug my shoulder in response.

Being practical I looked for pros and cons then decided that she should not have the baby. "Piyali you know I want this child but you know it is wrong, you cannot be a single mother and I cannot marry you now."

"There is no rescue than to quit this idea of keeping this child now but rather wait for us to settle down." I had tears in my eyes for losing a beautiful soul.

"You know you can be a good father." Piyali hugged me tight.

"And when does this happened?" said Akash aloud smiling and heading towards us.

"Mind your business." I smiled back.

"Congrats father." he taunted me.

"Shut up, we are settling down." I replied back.

"Marrying?" he questioned.

"Let's see." I knew I had no option.

"Anyways at least you told it yourself; well it was Piyali's plan."

"It is now two months since you people were in relationship and you didn't care to inform us."

"Told you na." I replied.

"Only when you need our help." Jenny too joined in.

"C'mon at least don't start now." I tried to court Jenny to bring her to my side.

"Whatever lets party now and Piyali tell him the truth?"

"Well I was joking, I am not pregnant it was just I wanted you to learn the lesson that your friends should know what ever is happening in your life."

"Oh I was scared let's switch to no glove no love policy." I laugh aloud and everyone present there laughed at my new policy.

An Ex Is Nothing Better than Having Sex

Finally after exams we broke up confessing everything like shit and it turned into a quarrel. It happened something like this…

+++*On a fine day for sex; as Love guru says: Play with her pussy, not her heart. But I was doing both here* +++

"This is the last time we are fucking." She reminded me.

"Yeah then I gonna lose this coziness of your vagina." I felt bad because from here I would be shifting to my hands before I could find a new place to park my manhood.

"So should we go for the last time?" she asked.

"As far as we are stick to the glove policy." I held her tight and kiss her tender lips.

Because of lack of time we started with a quick sex. I opened her t-shirt and she opened mine. I brutally opened her bra popping her breast out. Her nipples were hard ready to be caressed by my tongue. And then a lip lock happened as I push her body hard over mine and I droped her pants. I put my finger inside her panty and throw it down on the floor with one quick act like an experienced lover. I knew Piyali loves to have sex with pain and today it was a day when I was going to give her chronic pain. She responded well too and like a perfect girlfriend she dropped my pants taking my tool in her hand and pressing it a little to stimulate.

We started with kisses first. She kissed my forehead, I kissed her eyes, she kissed my nose, I kissed her cheeks, she kissed my chin, I kissed her lips, she kissed my neck, I kissed her ears, she kissed my chest, I kissed her armpits, she sucked my nipples and I in response kissed her nipples too; *the reddish brown nipples.*

+++ I knew this was the only pussy I could easily get +++

We looked into each other's eyes and then I lay on the bed. She came over me like a cowboy. I always loved to keep her on the top. I knew she always gave a perfect time when she was given the responsibility. She again kissed my chest and with her seductive eyes she gave me a bitchy look. I loved to see her in this act. I wished to click one of her picture like this. I put my hand on her head and pushed her down towards my dick. She got the signal. She obediently went down towards my dick and took it in her hand. She gave it a to and fro motion to it and smiled. I knew she was enjoying my thirst for her but she was not ready to quench it so easily.

"This is the last time." she moaned.

"Yes." I whispered, as I could hardly say anything.

"I will give you my best shot and I wish you to give yours." she put a deal.

Then she went down and licked the tip of my dick and sucks the red dickhead forcefully. With a few thrushes I found myself raping her mouth. As I held her hair to give her a throat choke, it was hard for me to control any longer and I blew in her mouth. Finally, I was over and now it was my turn to satisfy her with my best shot.

I threw her hard on the bed and opened the cupboard, searched for handkerchiefs. I tooks few of them and then went back to her. She still lay there waiting for me to be teased. She knew this time I was more into experimenting and she agreed.

I tied her to the bed with her legs apart revealing her privates openly. She never looked so much intense to the sex as she looked today. She found very seductive to be in my bondage. I then came over her.

"I want it more brutal"

"Brutal."

"Brutal, you know the meaning?" she cried and I as I looked into her eyes she looked as if the sex had overdosed her mind and she left her senses just for the gratification.

"Ok." I bored her with my eyes.

I went inside the bathroom and took hold of the paste. I then came over her and put the tooth paste over her vagina. It was so much helpful to keep her seduced.

"Fuck me hard." she cried aloud holding me and pinching with her nail. I felt pain as they dug deep into my skin and it bleed. But I was not ready to.

"You want it more brutal?' I asked.

"Can you go?" she asked.

"Yeah." I replied.

"Then go on you bastard." she screamed.

I this time went for search of candle. I lit the candle and put it there on the side. Then I came over her and inserted my solid into her privates. I knew she could not hold more. I stopped at once and then took hold of the candle.

I put hot wax over her nipples which were hard. She cried with pain but enjoyed it too. I again dropped another drop over another tit. She liked it more painful. Then I kissed her again all over her body and then dropped more wax over her. My rod was still inside her. I with my hand clear all the wax and sucked her red tits now. It was painful and as I looked into her eyes, she smiled. I in response started the momentum which took place for next 15 minutes and then I collapsed on her. She remained there in the position for next 30 minutes, and then I released her. She looked satisfied. Now it was time for us to share some after sex talks…

"So, it was nice."

"Way nicer than I expected."

"So finally this is a call for breakup." as I hold my clothes in my hands.

"Yes, the healthy one I guess."

"Hmm" I cleaned my sweat with her panty and then started wearing my clothes.

"But before we moved out from each other's life don't you think we should confess something to each other. Something like the mistakes we made being with each other so that next time when we have a relation with someone else we should know what we should not do.

"Ok, you first?" I was given this chance.

"To start with…" I start confessing.

1. I was peeing in your basin that day when you caught me.
2. I want to keep myself dirty and it's none of your business I love to be what I am. You better clean your character.
3. I used you as a sex toy for a good timer; please don't mind no glove policy was to take no trouble with you.
4. I love to fuck you several times but you are so boring in the bed. You never experimented with it. I mean the way I do.
5. Finally, the brutal confession; I never loved you, it was just for sex.

"I hope it haven't hurt you, now it your turn."

"Well…" She started confessing…

1. I was never your sex doll I knew we were fucking for fun; you were hardcore on me and I hated it. Love making and making love are two different things.
2. I hate the positions that you took while making out. C'mon be serious, that sex is sacred not a game. I wonder why you consider yourself a master of Kamasutra.
3. The first day you fucked me, dear you were shattered to know I was not a virgin which in fact I was till you fucked me and I was happy to hurt you.
4. I too never loved you so I don't mind getting fucked by you, I mean if you were fucking me I too was fucking you.
5. Take it as a compliment or an insult: You are an asshole and that's why I always say you are a dog; in fact all men are dogs, accept it.

Everything remained quiet for the next two minutes and then I broke the silence.

"Can I make love for one more time? Like a game. I will tell you how?" I smiled.

"I mean I feel so happy today that I was the one to whom you lost your virginity." I smiled witty.

"I always resisted this pose, let's try this today." I asked.

"Which one?" Piyali was excited too.

"Let's blind fold and go for 69." I suggested.

"Whatever but it will be the last time." she insisted, and then we blind folded ourselves and reached for each other's body. Her aura was awesome and I could feel her warmness on me. We slowly played with each other's body and enjoyed ourselves to the fullest.

And it happened for the whole night. We used each other's passion for the last time and quenched each other's thirst for sex. Piyali was a perfect partner for sex and before leaving her room; I wrote a short note for her and left my mobile. As Piyali woke up; my surprise was ready for her. She took the note and read it…

"Hope you love to be a porn star"

She quickly opened my mobile and searched for the video section. There she found a video renamed PIYALI MMS. She opened it wasting no time she played the video.

The video started with me reading out a message for her…

"Hello Piyali, I knew it that you will read the note and will search for this video; well, I know you must be thinking how bad I am that I made an MMS of you, but you are mistakenly wrong. I could be very bad to you, but I never did it to you. I may be your sex toy and enjoyed sex with you, but I respect you too at the same time."

"I respect you because I spent some time with you in bed, and I am very thankful to you that you trusted me to give room to me to enter your warm pussy."

"Keep good things in place. This mobile is a gift to you from me as I never gifted you anything when we were in relationship. Bye." and I was gone.

6

After sweet memories and time spent with Piyali; followed by a break up relieved me a lot. I was now not under the obligation, and a heavy heart that I was using this girl for sexual gratification.

So now it was clear from both the sides and we departed from each other's life. Days passed smoothly and I totally forgot about Piyali. And then…

Ring

"Hello."

"Hi." a reply came.

"Who is this?" I questioned.

"This is Akash here." said Akash from the other side.

"Oh! Hi Akash *bro* how are you?" I inquired, but I knew there was something more for which he had called.

"Are you coming to college? Our results have been declared." He asked without answering my senseless inquiries.

"Is it out?" I was nervous now.

"Yeah." The most predictable answer came.

"Meet you in 15 minutes" The plan to visit the college was made.

Entering college and without meeting anyone I ran towards the notice board where this result was displayed. I prayed to God before I looked for my name; as my exams had gone well, but still it was the final year. I had never studied, so for me passing was a tough job.

I started looking for the names in the notice board. I first looked for my name but could not find it. Suddenly Akash yelled aloud in happiness.

"I have got a first division." He shouted in exhilaration.

"Congratulations." I was very happy, but I was still looking for my name.

"How about you?" Akash was perturbed.

"Still could not find it." And now only the failure list was left to be confirmed.

"Piyali?" Akash asked.

"Fuck her I don't know" I was miffed.

"I think she has failed." Akash conformed as he pointed towards one of the names on the list failed students.

I smiled; I was happy for her, I don' know why. "Bastard you are laughing." Akash was confused watching me happy for her failure.

"I don't know why but she failed." I replied.

"Look for my result man." I ordered him now feeling confident.

"You too have failed." He answered as he looked at the other name in the same list where he found Piyali's name. I just cried out, "What the fuck is this?"

"This is not going to happen. I will talk to the principal about this." I said in despair.

I ran towards the principal's office.

"May I come in mam?" I asked for permission at the door as I reached the office.

"Yeah." She said.

"I failed but I think there is something wrong." I sounded nervous being in her room as a failed candidate.

"Go for a revaluation." She did not even care to look at me rather keeping her engaged in her work only.

"But…"

"I can't help; you can go." She gave her final answer, and I had no other option.

"Sorry." I excused myself and walked away from her room disappointed.

Suddenly I saw Piyali. As soon as I saw her, it was hard for me to face her; I ran toward the pillar out of her sight to hide myself. She went passing by me crying with her hanky in her hand. I smiled again.

"Girls." came from my mouth. I was now not sad for myself rather happy for Piyali.

"What you will do now?" Akash wanted to know.

"I will go for revaluation." I stuck to my decision.

"It will take time." Akash said.

"Until then I will enjoy my life." I gave him a callous answer.

"And Piyali?" he questioned.

"I don't know I don't care; she is not my girl friend anymore." I replied.

And then something happened. I was told to attend the classes so that I could have attendance for sitting in the next session for the supplementary session. And same happened for Piyali too, and I not at any time wanted to see Piyali's face but it happened, and it was not for now but for next three months.

1sy day of Supplementary class

I was avoiding Piyali and so was she. Suddenly the teacher entered, and Piyali had no other choice than to sit next to me.

"Who all are supplementary students here?" she raised the most pinching question.

I pointed towards Piyali. "And Siddharth you too." I was not redeemed this time.

"I will got through in revaluation." I was quite certain.

"Huh." Piyali gave the loser reflex.

"So who is going to discuss merchandise law?" she threw her second question.

I raised my hand. Piyali too raised her hand. And Piyali managed to answer it well.

"Can anyone answer common basket?" She kept on checking our knowledge.

I lifted my hand again.

"He can't even keep his socks in the shoe, how he can manage to talk about the forums and common baskets?" Piyali made comment at me, which was rather mean as it was I who was supposed to comment like this on someone's personal life.

"Mind your business and what about you?" I retorted.

"I pee in your basin actually I was masturbating; do you have a problem about it?" I became indecent in front of everybody.

"Loser." she responded.

"And that's why you are sitting next to me." I laughed and the whole class laughed along with me.

And then the teacher went from the class to the principal, as the fight turned stormier and it went into mother fucking scolding.

"What to do with you people?" The Principal asked.

"Go to the library, sit there and write an assignment on Microsoft Word in 1000 words on Accounts," and we were both penalized for our misbehaviors.

Both of us went to the library.

"I can do it better and faster." We started typing. I cut copy and paste it from Google where as Piyali kept on typing it from the textbook. And then I got an idea. I kick, the computer so that the power supply got disconnected and it turned off without getting saved.

"Hey you did it!" Piyali screamed.

"No I didn't actually I am done." I acted like a moron. She looked at my computer to verify.

"Stay away from me." I switch off my computer shutting it down.

I went to the principal's office; whereas Piyali kept on working there. In an hour, I was asked to meet the Principal.

"This is wrong Mr. Siddharth you have copied your work from the internet." I was caught for copying.

"I would not have noticed if Piyali hadn't told me," she continued. "Do it 10 times more but in your hand writing this time." I was punished again but more lethally this time.

I was now on fire. I went straight to Piyali. She was busy working on the computer. I put my hand on her chair and rotate it towards me and shouted at her as loud I could. "What the hell you do think of yourself." I shouted at her.

"I knew your IQ Sid you can only copy, and I told the truth."

"And you played fair game? How can you expect me to?" I replied in anger.

"*And don't teach your father how to fuck,*" I went dirty.

"Shut your dirty mouth." She too screamed back at me.

"C'mon accept it." She said again.

"Then why didn't you tell me the truth when we were in a relationship that you were using me?" I asked her.

"Bloody dog" she replied.

"Shit, you are a piece of an ugly shit." I tried to end it here.

"It's not your fault." I continued.

"I must say all men are dogs." She again said her usual lines.

And once again, we were sent to detain room as the Principal passing by caught us in the middle of the fight screaming at each other. The fight ended surprisingly as Principal told us that our desks would be near each other's in the supplementary exams. The ceasefire happened quickly without any moderator.

We both knew fighting would land us into more troubles. So right now this was the time that we should overcome hurdles together. Finally, we apologized and became friends again. But there was something we shared more often than friendship was the bed and this was something keeping us together. Finally, again this friendship turned into relationship and we started respecting each other as partners.

On a very good day, the revaluation result came and we had both passed. But before we breok up again, we decided to meet each other for the last time. We decided the venue to be our same old café lounge; one of the finest bars and kitchens in Delhi.

At Café 27
@
11:30 PM

The party was rocking and so were we. We took our seat after being exhausted for dancing from past three hours.

"Let's depart from here and make a new start." Piyali suggested smiling.

"Yes, let's not discuss this relationship again and not even mistakes we made throughout life." I replied.

"Yes, let's not talk about the pranks which you played on me that breathtaking prank the MMS story."

"Should we?"

"What?"

"Let's fuck, and fuck it for the last time." I gave a spontaneous answer.

She looked at me in agreement but still confused about the place; "Your place or mine?" I asked.

"Here" she replied back.

"What do you mean here?" I was confused as it was a public place.

"Let's move to the terrace." she took hold of my hand and took me to the terrace of the café's.

She took hold of a glass full of 90 ml without water. It was all dark and a little sound of the music was still audible.

"Let's fuck under the stars."

"It is safe?"

"Shut up and fuck me." She ordered.

And then in high spirits we started to kiss each other. The dress which she was wearing was a revealing one; I could easily see the notice her hard nipple's impressions on them. The breasts were just perfect cup shaped to hold and fondle. She made her move. She located my manhood with the GPS fitted in her hands and took hold of my nicely shaved balls. She took a sip of the Vodka and then kissed me spilling half of the liquor in my mouth. It tastes awesome and her hands kept moving over my dick. I felt myself under her control by now. She then kissed me on my lips again and smiled. Licking her finger she wet her lips and I knew she was ready for a blowjob.

I pushed her head down as she moved towards my dick opening the zipper of my trousers and revealing my dick to her. It was hard enough to be sucked by this woman. I took hold of the glass now. She started playing with her tongue and started sucking my dick. I could feel the thrust and the pressure; with few more to and fro shots I came in her mouth completely without warning her and I felt relaxed.

"Did you enjoy it thoroughly?"

"To its core."

"My turn, just suck my juices out of me," she offer me her vagina.

I was very excited to feel her cunt. I, wasting no time undressed her and made her lie on the terrace floor. It was all dark and by now the music had also stopped. I could hear the night cries of the dogs. I spread her legs exposing her crack, to get the perfect insertion of my tongue; and I finally started licking her juices. I cupped her vagina with my lips and sucked it hard. With few more sucks I felt the tightness in her body and finally she came spilling her juices over me.

"Are you a squirter?" I asked.

"Shut up"

"Get dressed up first before we talk about our experiences." she knew we were now going to talk about our sex experience to rate it as always.

She moved to get her dress.

"How do I look by the way?"

"Or I am just your sex doll as you always compliment me?" I could feel the pain of my last confession telling her to be my sex doll.

"Yeah you look great." I paused and complete my statement.

"When nude." I confessed.

"Is it a compliment or an insult?" she asked.

"Which way you think," I replied in a lighter note.

"There is something like outer beauty; this was what I was mentioning to you." She was not in a good mood.

"Well I compliment your inner beauty." I try flipping her useless queries cunningly.

"I mean look at these legs." I continued.

"Wow they look great." I pointed out her fish net tights over her beautiful legs.

"When do they open" I smiled at my witty prank.

"What do you mean, if I am sleeping with you that doesn't mean I am sleeping with someone else too." She sounded angry.

"Who can't judge a book by its cover?"

"By the way who are you to judge me" Piyali was angry and wanted to fight.

"A girl like you cannot judge me" I jumped out, wore my pants and searched for my shirt.

Like always I started the statement "Before we depart and never see each other's face any issues or anything you wanna say to me." I knew this would piss her off.

"I mean any advice?" she asked.

"Just be yourself Sid." It was the first time I saw Piyali so serious about me.

"And who is that Sid exactly?" I still could not find any answer to her words and was confused.

"The one who don't like 69, hates squirter and the one who is not an ATM," she replied back.

"You mean you kept me like an ATM machine." I was confused.

"Good for nothing more than money" I continued because it was more than what I could expect from her.

"No." she gave justification.

"Then what exactly does ATM means here?" I questioned.

"Well we use to call you ATM." she smiled.

"But why?" I was curious to know.

"And what's that ATM means here?" I questioned.

"It means Ass to Mouth."

"Fuck you hard, you called me this." I screamed in anger.

"Call me a dog if I will sleep with you again," I try adjusting my shirt.

"Fuck off that's what you want sex, a partner and then when it comes to emotions you are a real dog."

"It's not you who is a dog actually this is a problem with generations like you – I say all men are dogs and I stay high to my statement." She barked aloud while I move out of the terrace skipping the fight.

"And fortunately you are a king amongst them." She shouted more loudly as I bang the terrace door.

"What do you mean, with how many dogs are you sleeping." It was actually a slip of tongue in anger and I stood still.

Piyali slapped me hard on my face, before I could leave the place I tried to adjust for her misbehavior. I came back. "Come let me drop you to your house."

She said nothing but followed me. On the way home none of us spoke a single word.

+++*The sight was like a moment of silence, for every child we have lost from swallowing during a blow job.* +++

As we entered her house, she went to her bathroom I went to her table; there I found a sweet childhood photograph of hers. I took it along with me as I left her house. On the way I tore them down as revenge and barked; "If I am king amongst all the dogs then you are a bitch sleeping with me."

On the way back home with a new start I called Akash up for a rescue.

"Hello"

"Hi this is Siddharth, I need a rescue, help me out for your institution as I am late for the session. Make a way for my entry to your college."

"I will try it will be a monetary thing."

"How much?" I inquired.

"Let's look for a management seat." Akash replied.

"Okay message me if any are left."

Before I could reach home a message popped. "There are a few left, will message details tomorrow be ready with the paper work and the bank balance."

7

Frustrated at what had happened with me in the past I decided to start a new life where I wished to move ahead in my career. I decided to call Akash for a rescue.

Rings

"Hello."

"Hi." Akash replied.

"Akash you have forgotten me man."

"No dear I still remember you and your dirty jokes but I am unable to help you, you have to raise your budget." he went straight to the point.

"Right now I haven't told my dad that I failed so I am not short of money. I just need your help to get admission in your college. Talk to the management for the seat. I hope I can make it through I guess." I said.

"Okay let me use my father's sources. You know he is strict in these things."

"Ya but do help me and tell me how much I need to pay for."

A few days later something shitty happened I could not put together the sum that Akash told me, I was 2 lakhs short. With Akash's efforts finally we hit the jackpot.

"Hey man congrats! You made it to the college. Try and join the course as soon as possible. If you can come tomorrow with the desided money it would be best." It was the best news I had heard in my entire life.

Finally new phase life had begun. Piyali was a long gone story now. I needed a new girl to start a new life.

The first day at MBA College

I was a late student here and had missed an important part of any college, the orientation. I saw all kind of beautiful faces and heard unknown names. These beautiful smiles had a lot of dirty pasts at their back like mine. I knew they were all fakes, at least for the next few months till the real persons emerged.

It was attendance time and I had to play the most unwanted role. I was called upon by the teacher to the lecture stand for the introduction I had this stage phobia which I had to cope up with now. As soon as she said there were two more students who needed to be introduced, I was relived.

I went to the stage first and took hold of the mike as I was the only boy and the other two were girls. To my surprise, I saw Piyali standing next to me. I was hit by an iceberg dipped in the cold sea. My nerves flickered and my tongue froze, it was a bad start. I could not say anything other than my name "Siddharth" which I uttered with a lot of effort.

"Studied from…" and I stammered.

Everyone laughed and my first impression was a bad one. The girl on the first desk was confusing me with her cleaveage; as her boobs rested on the desk and at the same time she smiled while adjusting her specs; but it was un-enjoyable hurting. Every time I tried to say something this girl would press her assets with the desk laughing and luring me to search for the shape of her boobs and with the devil in my mind, I was rather distracted.

After the first disgusting class

"Did you look at the assets of that girl in the first row? Oh man just look at those tanks. Fuck man." I said adjusting my tool after the pee.

"Wash your hand and your mind, my dear friend." Akash replied.

"Piyali is here; try concentrating on your girlfriend." He futher suggested.

"What man you called Piyali too." I said depressed.

"Yeah I thought it will be a surprise for you. How was it? But you seem to be pretty unhappy." he patted my back.

"Wash your hand fucker." I retorted as he touched my neck.

"And.."

"We broke up, long back." I replied as I came out from the men's toilet and Jenny was waiting outside.

"She is not my kind of girl." I tried to explain.

"C'mon don't joke. You are not going to get any girl." Akash laughed.

"We have broken up." I said again, tring to make him understand that we had no chances.

"Again, but you people will reconcile we know." Jenny smiled, interrupting us.

"No man this is the end now." I tried to sound final.

"Even Piyali said so but we know you people will join again." Jenny again try to pacify me.

"After all sex sticks you hard." Akash smiled at his funny joke and we started moving towards the canteen.

"Just like this *samosa and the chatni*" he took hold of a samosa in his hand from the canteen counter.

"Leave it on the plate *babu*." said the canteen boy.

"Okay okay." Akash replied back.

"No we are way apart" I tried to explain.

"This is not the matter of *samosa and chatni* but think about a *pizza and the chatni*."

"We are like good food wrongly presented." I explained.

"You love her, accept it." said Akash to me as he sat down on one of the chair's in the canteen.

"C'mon it's the truth" Jenny also sat down adjusting her perfect butt.

"Think again." said Akash and Jenny together.

"Yes think." said the canteen boy.

"Who are you?" All three of us asked him.

"Samosa garam hai laau chatni ke sath." said the canteen boy. We all laughed at once looking at him.

"Ek try to banta hai." said Jenny to me.

"None from my side, I mean how many times." I replied.

"One last." Akash forced me this time with his words.

"May be but we are through." I gave my final reply and acted stubborn. I hit my fist hard on the canteen table and everyone looked at me. I was stunned for a while, then took my bag and went out to have fresh air.

While moving out I saw Piyali entering the canteen. She gave a loser stare to which I responded the same way. And the stare continued for next two minutes until Jenny took hold of the situations. I knew Piyali was also in the mood of taking revenge on me; her blame game was on so was mine.

Confessions of a dirty mind

I was in search of revenge. All I needed was my first plan to be executed and with God's grace I got this chance very soon. In the first week we were told to buy a new laptop as it was a part of the curriculum to work on the word and power point files.

Everyone got a new laptop with their own money; for boys it was processor, RAM and ROM quality that mattered and for girls it was red, pink or white.

For the work we met at Piyali's room

"Shit man my laptop crashed" said Jenny disappointed.

"What happened?" Akash questioned.

"Virus; your pen drive has a lot of viruses in it." She screamed.

"You installed it?" Akash tried to save himself from the allegation.

"Why did you try to execute something you don't know?" he continued.

I kept listening to their conversation and in a minute or two I was asked to settle their fight.

"So what is the charge? What exactly has happened?" I wanted to clarify.

"He gave me a pen drive and it had virus in it and it went into my boot setup of Laptop."

"And now it is crashed, I lost every file and even assignments." she continued with a sad face.

"She must have clicked some miscellaneous folder or program."

"He was carrying a virus it went itself." The fight took a bad turn.

"Itself?" Akash too was screaming loud now.

"Yes this is some kind of self executive program."

"Oh I see," and an idea struck my mind.

"Surrender this pen drive to me I will handle it till then, you try to fix it or else I will have to arrange." I took hold of the pen drive.

I took the pen drive and now it had to be plugged into Piyali's laptop. It was a fine idea. I waited for the next two days till my turn for presentation came. I was ready to skip it as I was new in the class and was not good at the topic. To drown with your enemy was a perfect blend here.

That day, I went to the college discharging my laptop and leaving its charger. I knew Piyali must be carrying one as it was my day for presentation.

"Mam my laptop is not turning up can I please postpone this presentation to next week?" I asked.

This was enough for Piyali to give her laptop and make her point in front of the whole class. I too cunningly inserted the pen drive in it and my mission of gifting her a virus was accomplished.

"Where is the presentation Mr. Siddharth?"

"I cannot find it here mam." I put on a worried face cunningly hiding my bad intentions.

"You haven't made it I know." She tries to scratch truth.

"You are a dull guy." she continued.

"Give me one chance mam" I pleaded.

"We can't give any chances here, we are not allowed. Let's see if possible in the end of all the presentations; till then you will be marked zero."

Piyali was happy on hearing the word zero but it was a remark for me because I was planning for the next big thing. Piyali was working on her thesis and I knew she had no backup plans. And now there wasvirus was ther in here machine giving me a chance of pure victory.

Few hours later in a free class...

"Mam I want to give this presentation", just an introduction to what Siddharth is supposed to present. Actually last night I studied about it so it is still there in my laptop."

"You?" mam was confused.

"Okay go on." Piyali felt blessed.

"Before this presentation begins, I would like to tell you I have two types of students in this institution. First type who are not doing their work right and will be taken charge of it at the time of internals and other who are showing responsibility, like this student who is standing here and will give a presentation on which Siddharth was supposed to give." After her lecture she looked at me angrily. I kept quiet.

Piyali fixed the laptop and started the projector. The first slide appeared on the screen, as I looked at the designing. And as she started giving the presentation, I noticed the presentation was mine and shit happened. We all were forced to sit in the class with a presentation.

"Hey this is my presentation." I retorted.

"Shit down" one of my classmate told me to keep mum.

I looked at him. He was someone who always tried to be bossy and make impressions on teachers showing him to be superior to other.

"Silence" the teacher said.

And finally with the last slide the show ended.

"Thank you miss." The teacher looked at Piyali.

"Piyali." She uttered her name.

"Good attempt and I must say you are now in good books of teachers." she smiled and left the class.

"Congratulations." Everybody congratulated her.

I looked at her like a culprit and she gave me a piteful smile. I knew it was my trap in which I had got fucked. I knew my next step which had to be bigger and it didn't take much time to me to crash her hard disk finally damaging her thesis work which did not have backup. Piyali knew I had done but it was a tit for tat game and niether had any sympathy for the other.

Anyhow she was in the good books of teachers which came as a good luck to her. She was helped by many teachers and her thesis finally got approved for the second year to work upon on the mercy grounds.

Rains and Tears are Dangerous

The first year went smoothly till it rained; it was time when we started ignoring each other in the class after the examination and concentrated more on studies. I was in a friendship with the BBW – big breast woman, the first bencher girl. She lured me with those big tanks and Piyali was on her own trip. Moreover our specialty class kept us away from each other most of the times. One day on the way home on my bike it started raining. I wanted to enjoy the first summer rain. I kicked my bike and rode it from the college. As I passed the gate of the College I saw Piyali waiting for the bus. I felt like the time had frozen at that moment. This was the first time I enjoyed watching her, in clothes. She was in her proper college dress. But today she was looking different. I gazed upon her but did not find myself comfortable. I saw her from an angle and the time slowed down more as I passed her. Going a little distance I decided that I had to look at her again. I had no reason why I was thinking like this but I took a turn. I knew I was doing wrong to myself I could fall in love again, but today I wanted to love her. I didn't know why it was happening to me but I was in a dangerous situation helpless.

I could hear the sound of a million rain drops pouring on this mother earth and soothing as they touched my face too. I could smell and taste rain and love. Yes love was in the air. As I returned I reached her she was still struggling to catch a bus. I stopped my bike to look at her with a little wicked smile thinking should I ask her for to take a lift or not. I was confused. Love has a tendency to confuse anyone. She was the one I loved in childhood and had 2 break ups before I could meet her again.

Suddenly Apoorv with Akash and Jenny came in the car. Apoorv was a secret admirer of Piyali and her former boy friend, asked her if she cared for a lift and she took the advantage. I followed her a little and then with the next light on the road I went my way. It was a rumor that Piyali and Apoorv were going out and today I had seen it. But Jenny and Akash going along with them was a little hurting too.

+++ *As Love Guru says: Cheating is easy. If you really want a challenge, try being Faithful.* +++

After few hours at Jenny's Place

"What a bitch she is," I screamed aloud in anger reminding myself of the incident that took place today.

"Whom are you talking about?" Jenny questioned.

"Your friend." I gave a bitter reply.

"You mean, Piyali."

"Yes."

"What did she do to you?" Jenny was confused.

"You hardly talk to each other now." she continued.

"Nothing." I tried changing the topic now.

"C'mon didn't you see Jenny, Piyali was talking so nicely to Apoorv, as if she was inviting him," Akash came to my rescue.

"Yeah, that's what I am talking about." I too joined.

"I mean if she knew that Apoorv like him, then why is she playing games with him?" I continued.

"Yes." Akash too gave his view.

"And when you knew that you and Piyali were playing with each other, why did you both end up like this. I mean why you broke up with a fight, why not on a happy note." Jenny's voice was high.

"And you are enjoying your life with some other girl, why you are so much concerned about Piyali." she hit me at the right place where it could hurt me the most.

"As a friend." I rescued myself.

"Friend!" she stretched the word.

"You hurt her." she continued.

"Who me, I saw her with Apoorv today okay. It was way hurting for me." I went straight.

"And what about her, when you are going along with that other girl in the class?"

I looked at Akash.

"You will say this because you are supposed to be her friend." Akash reacted.

"Male chauvinism."

"*This is not about male dominance and female innocence.*" I smiled.

"I don't want to talk any further on this." She stood up in anger.

"Stop." Akash straighten his leg to block her way.

She pushed his legs away and went towards the door.

"When you girls don't win you try to manipulate."

"What am I manipulating Akash? said Jenny in tears.

"Have the conversation then." It was first time Akash was shedding his frustration.

Further during the talk with Akash and Jenny over this issue conflicts came up between them also. And finally the most unexpected thing happened. Akash and Jenny broke up like us.

8

Jenny had no one for company. So, she and I become close. I had been her best friend for so many years now. The last fight had ended her relationship with Akash but they both looked happy.

++ + As it is wisely said: Sometimes breakups are important to add value to people and the love between them. Breakups and make ups are the part of life +++

They were both giving time to each other to reconsider things before they patched up again. Their relationship had become so monotonous with time that this exercise was necessary.

But for me, my relationship with Piyali had frozen. I hated her for not loving me. For me, if I let did not make a difference. What stung was seeing Apoorv with Piyali

"Is Piyali going around with Apoorv?" I asked Jenny to confirm the rumor.

"What do you have to do with it?" she questioned back.

"Nothing just conforming." I smiled.

"Your thesis presentation is coming; I believe. You must be prepared for it." Jenny suggested.

"Already done Jenny." I patted my back.

"Any plans for Piyali?" She asked. She knew I would be cunningly planning anything to get even with her.

"Will ruin her one day." I blurted out unintentionally.

"We all know you crashed her hard disk." She stared.

"This time more storms will blow oven her." They reply came straight from my heart.

However, I was wrong this time. I never knew that something was coming my way rather I was heading towards it.

Piyali was all set to ruin me like the way I that ruined her presentation. On the very day of the presentation it was raining on and most of the students were absent.

My presentation began. As I clicked the pen drive option on my laptop with the projector connected, I could hardly find my presentation in it. Rather it contained a few porn movies whose icons were perceptible with a few naked women in a gang bang pose. It was a dishonor for the Institute where I was studying. I was expelled for the next 15 days to which I could do nothing than to say sorry. However, this time it was more than anticipations. I knew Piyali didn't do it herself Apoorv was involved somewhere.

I made a plan to do something drastic Apoorv. I knew he loved Piyali a lot and this was a key factor to break him down. Either I should propose Piyali, or I needed someone to do that for me. I had no one to help me other than Akash.

"Help me out." I asked Akash.

"This isn't funny Sid." Akash replied.

"All you have to do is make Apoorv believe that Piyali is going out with you. The rest I will handle."

"No" he refused flatly.

"Yes." I tried to make him agree.

"No, I won't do anything like that." he stuck to his decision.

"You are a devil, bastard" he continued.

"Come on I bow, you fuck me. What else can I offer you?" I begged.

"Look; Jenny is out of town for a week. You have to do nothing. This will be a favor to me." I pleaded finally compelling Akash to help me out of the mess.

Rings

"Hey Piyali today is my birthday, and I have a small party at CCD; I hope you don't mind joining me in?"

"C'mon happy birthday, at what time is the party??"

"5 o'clock today."

"Jenny will be there *na?*" She asked.

"Yeah she will be there…" Akash lied.

"But she is out of town." she confirms.

"She is coming straight at five, right on time."

CCD @ 5

I made the arrangements for Akash. Finally, 15 minutes later Piyali entered, and she looked stunningly beautiful. I called

Apoorv and cooked a story, about the reason why I and Piyali broke up. She was fond of cocks, and now she was going out with him and Akash too. To give a flavor to the story I called him right to the spot to see it with his eyes.

"Where is Jenny?" Piyali asked Akash.

"She is on the way." Akash lied.

And as I prepared for Akash, a cake came with "I LOVE YOU PIYALI" written on it.

Akash bent at the knees with a rose in his hand showing her care for her. This was not part of the story, but his over acting was very good. I smiled as I showed Apoorv the right. Piyali was confused at this act.

"What is this Akash?" she was all puzzled.

"I really love you." Akash finally advanced toward the girl.

"I can't do this to you; you are my good friend, and Jenny is my friend too."

"Think about us together."

Apoorv could not hear anything, but the gesture was simple enough to believe.

"I will fuck this girl right here." Apoorv said in anger and this could ruin the story.

"Hey stop." we will take revenge jointly in the right way. She is a very cunning girl; look at Akash, he is my best friend and what he is doing behind my back," I blamed Akash for it in front of Apoorv.

"Think of us together." Akash said to Piyali.

"I can't and if Jenny comes to know about it then it will be hurtful for all of us." said Piyali.

"Who all, Jenny has broken with me up." Akash gave a statement.

"Jenny will be hurt, you are not thinking and Sid." she said confused.

"Sid?" Akash tried to believe what he heard.

"No I am going. This is it; this is your day, Happy B'day." Piyali left the place.

"Thank you for coming." Akash greeted.

"Are we together?" Asked Akash.

"Yeah, may be." Piyali replied.

Wasting no time I met Akash to hear his version the whole incident.

"Thank you Akash." I smiled.

"We are together, thanks to you. You gave me courage to propose to the girl I adore. Don't take it personally." Akash put his hand on my shoulder.

"What??" I looked at him like a fool.

9

Piyali was far smarter than us. Well, us here were Apoorv, Akash and I. A few days after the story begin with Akash and Piyali. Jenny came back to the scene.

"What shit am I hearing Akash?" She created a scene in the college.

"Piyali and I are together." said Akash, holding Piyali's hand.

"No we are together." Piyali left Akash's hand and took hold of Jenny's hand.

Now it was clear that the girls were at the same end.

"He told me to propose." Akash look at me and winked.

"We were just playing with you. I knew Piyali would say it to you, and you will be running back. I missed you." Akash had no choice.

"She is like my sister." He wriggled out of it now.

"And why the hell you are playing with someone's emotion Sid." Jenny cried aloud in anger. Jenny was a good friend of mine; I had never seen her in so much anger.

As I saw Apoorv coming, I played another ace.

"Apoorv told me what you have to say about Piyali." I asked.

"What do I have to say about this whore?" he said what was in his mind about her after what I had showed him.

"Hey stop, bastard what do you think?" Jenny threw her anger at him. It was enough for me to save my skin and change the topic. I took Apoorv to the other end and Akash took hold of girls to other end. Akash knew this was the only way out for us.

"Chill brother this thing has messed up. We have terminal exams to clear. Let's not get messy here. We will resolve it outside the campus." I tried my best to convince Apoorv, and he left the place.

I went to Jenny and Piyali, "Look he told me to track you down as he was in love with you, and wanted to check on you" I cooked another story.

"Now please don't call him or message him. Look at his bloody attitude." I pointed at Apoorv.

"Okay let's go to the canteen." Jenny ended the fight from her side.

"What about me Sid?" Akash messaged me on my mobile to rescue from Jenny.

"Jenny... Jenny... Jenny... my dear friend if you happened to love him and have a fear of losing him, please reconcile." I told her.

"I played it double timer to get Akash involved and make you feel his importance."

"Now don't waste your time and be just like a good boyfriend and girlfriend." I looked both of them.

"Oh Akash" Jenny hugged him tight.

"Hey, just move from here." Piyali suggested as they both were creating a scene there.

As we entered the canteen, a message popped up on my mobile's screen.

"Nicely played and if Jenny would not have been involved, I would have shown you who I am" It was a message from Piyali.

"Thanks." I texted her back.

"Anyways; thanks to you Sid, for Apoorv." I smiled looking at her.

2 months passed after our first exam

The first year of college passed so quickly that we hardly noticed how time passed. We all secured good marks and I got zero in all my presentations, adding one more zero in my life.

However, before we try hard our luck for the college selection it was time for an Industrial tour. We all were sent to Bangalore for the visit. Tickets were booked and we were told to assemble in our college premises. From her we had to start our journey. Everyone seemed to be very happy. Exams had done something good too for a few people like Jenny and Akash.

Afraid of failing in the exams, Akash bent again and said sorry to Jenny, and she readily accepted to help him in studies. They studied together and passed. Jenny and Akash helped me.

The tour

Akash was Jenny's new servant I must say. This could be noticed easily from the way they both were treating each other, something like fresh boyfriend and girlfriend. As I could see him carrying her bags and even her handbag too and it was a real shameful act. But still Akash looked great doing it.

The tour started and so did our first fight. We all knew it was a hard time travelling in a train if you have a lower birth. Everyone would join and keep occupying your seat, so to rest was next to impossible. Piyali and I were adjusted to one set. We had to decide who would take the lower berth and who would take the upper one. I kept my stuff on the upper berth and went to pee. As I came back I could not find my stuff there. Piyali was sitting in my place as an act of reading a weird love novel. I saw her dig into the book. I tried searching for my stuff then in anger.

"Where the fuck is my stuff?" I screamed in anger.

"Lower berth." she replied.

"This is my berth; I am taking the upper berth." I cried aloud, but she kept herself engrossed in the book. She knew I could not do anything. All I could do was to scream.

Jenny and Akash, on the other hand, kept themselves busy. They knew if they land got involved in our fight, it would shift to them too.

"I want my seat back." I screamed again letting the two lover bird to hear that I was saying anger.

"Why are you screaming?" Jenny asked.

"Look Jenny, she has taken my seat." I try to shield myself.

"You can take her's *na*, after all there are plenty of them." she pointed me one seat.

"I want an upper berth" I cried like a kid; I knew I was looking senseless.

"Why don't you take this one?" she pointed towards Akash upper berth.

"Take this one man and for God sake give a rest to this fight." Akash started shifting towards my berth; he knew I had no other option but to adjust. I took Akash's seat silently.

In the evening mam came in for attendance and after that it was time for *Masti*.

"Let's play **a word from my heart** game." suggested Jenny.

"What's that?" Akash inquired.

"What we have to do is to write a word in a chit, and afterwards, we have to mix and throw them all. One by one we will pick it and later will say a name and open for a word.

We took our seat in a circle. Our other classmates too joined in. All of us took pen and paper.

"Let's write one word."

And the game started. I wrote "Moron" and threw my chit. Now it was time to pick up one chit and started the game.

"Let's now pick it." We all took hold of one chit and started to read.

"For you Akash." Jenny said while opening the chit she choose.

"What?"

"Moron" we all laughed aloud; Piyali knew it was my chit.

"Your turn Piyali." said Jenny

"And this is for Sid." she continued.

She opened and read "**secret admirer**" and then we all laughed again.

Now it all went with Jenny to Akash and Akash to Jenny with all the dirty words we could find and Jenny and Akash wrote them for themselves came to our side and each of them had love quotation in them.

We all knew who was writing for whom. After few hours, we took our berths and turn off the light. I could hear the sound of Akash and Jenny talking and I could easily find Piyali awake. Her eyes were glittered in the dark and I could find her looking at me. I too looked into her eyes and asked by blinking my eyes at the other side. I could hear Jenny and Akash kissing under my berth. Then I looked at Piyali she smiled and asked me with her eyes to come over there to see what these fellows were doing. I made a move; I slowly jumped from my seat to her and went into her sheets. I lay side to her and she put her head on my chest and we both started looking at them.

I could find the pelvic movement for their fuck which was getting more intense with each dip. Piyali kept her hand on my stomach and hugged me hard. I knew she was feeling high looking at them fucking so passionately, I too was high all I need was a start from Piyali's side to fuck her and finally, she gave in.

She forgot that we were not in a relationship and suddenly like always her hand went down on my pants over my dick. It remained there for a while. It was all dark. I could feel her pumping heart, and I knew she wanted me and my hot rod. I gave a little stroke to my dick over her hand cradling her into my arms. Her fist grabbed my dick over the pants, and she started her part of seduction. She kept moving her fist up and down and I too initiated the strokes by moving my groin.

I then guided her hand into my pant and let it over my dick from inside. She took hold and just like an obedient girl she started to give a master stroke. I felt relieved and then I shed my cum on her hand. My body froze for a while with her hand still inside my pants. Then slowly without spoiling my clothes, she removed her hand and kept it outside. I could see her hand wet with my sperm.

"Taste it, I bet this is the best juice you would have ever tasted" I whispered.

She looked at me for a while and then she gave a try by touching her tongue to the juice.

"Not good yet not so bad." she replied.

"Mine is best." she smiled.

I put my hand in her panty to which she responded by unbuttoning her pants and lifting her buttock to put it down. I then put my finger in her crack to get a little of her juices. It was filled with it, ready to get fucked. I then tried to find her G- spot finally, I got the heaven. I pressed her G- spot a little to which she moaned. I knew she loved it. The intensity of my vibrations over her pussy, and her moans increased with every brush I made with my finger, and finally; she contracted her whole body, and then she relieved. We both felt exhausted so I lay there and wondered when we fell asleep hugging each other.

At dawn to change places Jenny woke up and found me and Piyali under the same sheets. She smiled looking at her two favorite bastards fucking each other but everything remained same in the day.

"For this reason you bastards need the upper berth," Jenny called Akash to show us positioned together under the sheets silently sleeping after satisfying each other. My hand was still in her crack and the sperm was still spilled over Piyali's hand.

"Shh…" let them enjoy and he grabbed Jenny from her butt for another morning fuck round.

Sex was the glue to keep us together. We knew once we had started we would be doing it all the way in the journey, and it happened.

Finally on the way back home at the last hour of the journey, on the door a few miles away from the destination.

"So are we the same ones who were fighting or have we changed after all these fucks for the day and night have turned us into a relationship?" she asked.

"If fucks have the capability to solve the problems, if it had, if it was, I would have done it long before." I replied smiling sneakily.

"That's what I am clearing here. I mean we are doing it with no responsibilities. I hope you too, think the same." I continued.

"I do; I know. We are together until it helps both of us. Let's not convert it into a relation and drag it until it breaks up like as always," she said monotonously.

"It happened and happened, let's not end it in a good note. Not like always telling each other's faults. Let's end it here smiling" I smiled to which she also responded, and we hugged each other.

For once I thought of throwing her from the door but I controlled myself and gave her way to her seat. It just reminded me of a great man, who wisely said…

+++ *Don't fuck your enemy with the sword, if you really want to fuck them, rather fuck them with your dick* +++

Back to the College

Now we had no exams, it was just thesis to be selected and finally with few amendments it worked fine. We all knew our hard work which was now preparing us to work in the corporate sector. We were the new bulls in the market.

Back to the college and a few surprises were ready for us. Looking at the notice board we found few placements to be held from which one of the highly reputed one was from the banking sector. It was from Kokum Bank, one of the leading banks and it was my target apart from my bad results in academics. I knew something more than presentations, score and Interview was needed, and it was my confidence.

"Hey I think this chance is just for me!" she said to one of her friends while I was imagining myself in the bank.

"I think this is for me too." I replied looking back at her.

"First go and get a good score in presentations." She laughed along with her friend.

"Are you challenging me?" I looked at her with anger.

"No, I don't think you are up to the mark for a challenge; average scorer." she complimented me with an insult.

Interviews were held, I participated in all three rounds and then we went away as the term ends. A time came when no one remained in contact with another. The fights with Piyali were long forgotten. Akash was now not a part of my daily routine and the eye tonic Jenny was seriously an issue, but porn helped me a lot out here.

As someone asked Love Guru, "Which is more dirty sex or talking about sex?"; he replied: Nothing is dirty about sex until you have the art of imagining it, rest all your imagination, hands will do +++

From College to Work

As the Interview went fine for me, I was confident that I would get selected. It was the first time I did not stammer and managed to show my confidence. The biggest deal was out and I was a contender against the rest. But for me it was Piyali.

Finally, on a very fine morning rather we can say on a lucky morning, I received a mail from the Bank. I opened the letter and to my surprise it was a job offer with five zeroes amount per annum. For a fresher it was a treat. I was happy. Wasting no time, I called Jenny and Akash for the good news.

On the first day of the work

I was ready to start a new journey. To be very frank, Jenny was a very good friend, Akash was my team mate and Piyali did not mean anything to me. I was in a new life and they meant nothing to me now.

The day came when I had to join the job. I took the appointment letter with me and got ready to my best. The place where I had to join was not very far from my place. After about half an hours' drive I reached the building. As I entered the building of Bank, I adjust my tie and went straight to the manager's room, wasting no time to make my first appearance on time.

I looked at the girl at the desk there, she was awesome. I made up my mind that she would be the next. I looked at her in such a way she smiled as she was taught to smile for the clients, I smiled back. She was awesome. She was dusky with the perfect shapes to lure men like us. She had a very odd taste about dressing and the bangles added to her beauty. I noticed that she had only one ear ring on. It got my attention.

"I have the appointment letter." I showed it her.

"Siddharth." she read out loud.

"Friends call me Sid." I tried to be more frank with.

"Trisha." She introduced herself, her voice was seducing.

"Mr. Madhur, our boss is waiting for you inside. Get yourself introduced to your co- workers too. You can find me here all the time."

"By the way, what about the ear ring?" I was curious to know.

"Well most of the people don't notice. Only those who look hard can notice." she flirted on the first day.

"Just one." she smiled and pointed towards Mr. Madhur's cabin. I entered knocking on the door first.

"Sit down, Mr. Siddharth." Mr. Madhur offered me a seat.

It was hard for me to judge him at first sight but my experience with such men were always challenging. He had a crooked nose with a disturbing smile as if he knew what was there in my mind. He seemed to be pretty much involved in office politics.

"Meet your new colleague." He introduced to me a lady next to me on whom I hadn't noticed before taking my seat.

"Hello." I turned to wish her.

"Hello." It was Piyali and we shook hands.

"D.E.S.T.I.N.Y." I tallk to myself.

10

Waiting in the rain for the light to turn green, I was just a few minutes away from the office. I knew I was late but had to wait for 30 more seconds helplessly as I looked at the waiting time. It was raining heavily and it was tough to drive. Finally I reached office 20 minutes late.

"Mr. Madhur is calling you in his cabin." I was notified by Trisha as she passed me touching me with her hand unintentionally.

"Is he angry?" I asked.

"You are late as always." She replied.

This was the first time I was late for a valid the reason earlier I had been late due to my faults. But today I knew nothing could help me and I had to cook some good story. As I entered Mr. Madhur's cabin my heart beat fast, as if I was going to my college practical. I had never felt so nervous.

"May I come on sir?" I asked for permission and found Piyali already sitting there.

I was pretty sure that Piyali must have said something

regarding my absence in the office. I felt angry but today was her day.

"So Mr. Siddharth, and Piyali you too; as you are the two newest joiners in the bank, I would like to give you an opportunity to pat your back. I am a right-handed person so you must be knowing it I will pat just one only." He smiled uttering his lame dumb self-centered theory of how wonderful and ambitious he was.

"I gave you this opportunity so that you both would work on the field for the bank for the next 15 days and help me; I want the bank to gain a little momentum regarding the accounts."

"In simple words I need more people opening their accounts in our bank." he said.

I was looking his way with fishy eyes; I knew that this must be his stake in his job. That was why he is putting us in somuch field work. I stood there along with Piyali.

"What are you two people looking at? Move... move ... go to the field now, I need results..." He shouted, and we moved quickly out of his office.

Both of us went straight to front desk and asked Trisha for the papers works and forms. "Wear these cards." Trisha handed us two cards. It seems like we were planned for this exercise.

"These are the details, just revise them and start the job." she smiled at me.

I knew like me Trisha too fantasized about me. Whenever I used to think about her, I could imagine her in lingerie wearing a police cap with stilettos.

She was a perfect blend of reductions and femininity. I could imagine her *kamasutra* poses. Tearing myself off from day dreaming, I went to work.

Two days and no entry, I could not find any convincing customer.

"Any new account?" Trisha asked me as I stood next to her desk.

"No wonder, Is this bank going to close?" I shed my despair with my words.

"You need to focus." she consoled as she touched my hand. A spark of desire ran through my body.

"Take these three numbers, these are queries for the account; I am handling these to you, and I wish this thing remains only between us." I looked at her; she smiled. I took the slip and dialed the number, and received a positive response. Within a few hours around six when it was closing time for the bank, I was way ahead to the target from Piyali. Outside the office building I met Trisha.

"Did it help you?" Trisha asked.

"Thanks a lot."

"Join me for Coffee." I asked her for the first time like a friend.

"We can think about it." she leaned over me.

Then we headed towards the nearby Café and ordered two Irish coffees, and started to talk.

"Piyali was your girl friend and now you people don't even talk?" she asked, confirming to rumors she must have heard.

"She was, not now." I answered.

"Never seen you with your boyfriend?" I said without delay.

Her eyes went wet, "Sorry." I tried to console her without knowing the reason why she was crying.

"No it's okay." She swipes her tears with her hanky.

I took hold of her hand "Have water?" I try to show sympathy.

"It's okay. I am fine."

"Let's not spoil this time."

"You know ever since you entered the office, I have a little crush on you." she leaned me towards.

+++ *Wise men says if she tells you that she love you, tell her to join the club.* +++

"They say it has alcohol in it?" I asked her to substantiate and changed the topic.

"That's why you ordered two of these." she smiled.

"I mean you thought you will make me high and take my advantage." She continued.

"No, I did not mean that." I assured her.

"Think why I helped you; there might be a good reason?" She puzzled me.

"And the reason is?" I asked as I knew the answer.

"I am already fallen for you and you are still thinking." She held my hand and took near her breasts and I could feel the warm softness.

"It has been raining since morning and I haven't enjoyed myself at all." She stared at me; I too gave a helping look.

+++ *As Love guru says: Jo mile kha lo, kal kisne dekha, more over beggars are not choosers* +++

Then she took my out in the rain. She was very happy getting wet in the rain. I looked at her from the side. She was dancing in the rain. Her assets were clearly visible and were wonderful to watch. Her cleavage was huge as I just noticed as her clothes clung to her body.

"Come in the rain." She asked me to join her.

"No, No." I refused.

"C'mon." she then took hold of my hand and ever since I left my teenage, this was the first time I was under the little pouring drops. I felt so romantic; it was something missing from my life.

"Let's move." I asked her to leave the place now as it was getting late, we headed towards my car.

"No, I want to enjoy myself a little more." Said Trisha like a little girl.

"Let's have some tea you are all wet, you might catch a cold."

Trisha look at herself, she was really all wet and transparent. She kept quiet. Suddenly she covered herself with her hands. I noticed her covering herself. I took hold of her hand and took a bold step.

"Friends?" I smiled expressing my thirst for her.

"Yeah." she replied back giving me a way.

"Leave it as it is." I looked the other side and then she felt comfortable. Then we went on a long drive and on the way I intentionally touched her thighs while changing the gear. She too did not mind my touch.

On the drive I could still find Trisha adjusting herself as her clothes were all wet. I could see her tits clearly as they were hard. Suddenly, she opened the dashboard case of my car, and she found vodka.

"Hey, Siddharth what's this?" She asked with the bottle in her hand.

"Vodka." I replied.

"Can I have a sip?"

"As you wish." I tried to sound innocent.

As soon as I gave permission she gulped a few ml and in around fifteen minutes, vodka made her high.

"Do you love me?" asked Trisha drunken.

"Sit straight Trisha." I tried to make her sit straight as she had fallen on my lap.

"What if I touch you here, haven't you been watching me with your lusty eyes for the past six months."

"You had fantasies about me; I had seen you adjusting your pants looking at me."

"Let me take you to your place" I took a turn for her place.

On the way I reached a lonely place, she hugged me tightly. I was a bit confused and it was unexpected. I remained silent and enjoyed her heat. Then she did something more unexpected. She bent down in the car, and unzipped my pants without even asking me like a slut. I kept driving enjoying the whole thing. She then took hold of my dick and started sucking it hard. I took the vodka and make a large gulp and started enjoying the ride. She kept on increasing the momentum and I gulp more of Vodka neat. As I stopped at the signal, I closed my eyes and passed in her mouth. She lay there and I just hung on to my seat for a while. I could not believe what happened a minute ago.

As I opened my eyes I saw Piyali in a nearby car smiling at me. I was shocked looking at her and afraid of what I had done.

"It happened unintentionally." I replied looking at her without being asked.

"It's okay." she smiled again.

"No I mean it happened and I repent." I said again.

Suddenly, Trisha moved up with my shirt adjusting her and came upward.

"Who are you talking to?" She asked looking at the other side.

"Piyali." I uttered the name.

"But who is here, where is Piyali?" She asked.

"Here." I pointed at the other side but I could see no one.

"Let's go, let me drop you at your place." I tried changing the topic.

She remained quiet on the way and in five minute we reached near her building and finally Trisha broke the silence.

"You know Sid, you can fuck me anytime, and you can fuck a hell of lot of women."

"But one thing I must say, you are in love and whenever and who-so-ever you fuck will be a sin."

"I can see love in you for Piyali" I did not respond to her drunkard talk. I kept silent.

"Good night."

"Think about what I said, admit it and went to her, apologize and reunite." She suggested.

"Good night." and I raced the car.

Something had changed since then with Trisha and me; I was not fairer to her. With her help I finally succeeded to win this battle but I knew somewhere I was lost which I was not admitting. I never wanted to love her…

11

Office and the routine

"Fast." whispered Trisha in my ears as I pumped my body lifting her leg over the basin in the ladies toilet.

I gained momentum. We were in a public toilet near our office. I always wondered why Trisha was so much fun doing sex. She was one of the convincing bitches a guy could fuck in the middle of the city with no fear. She knew well where and where not to; and with no fear and rejections.

I just loved fucking her and it was now regular between me and Trisha. I wonder why she was so much support to me but my question always remained the same while fucking her.

"You didn't' tell me about your boyfriend?" I asked Trisha while my dick waspumping hard.

She remained quiet as always.

Taking a few more minutes I finally came inside her. She took her hanky from her purse and washed my dick and zipped my pants. Suddenly, someone entered the toilet and I hid myself along with Trisha in one block. I sat on the commode and lifted my legs so that my shoes would not be visible.

"A little fast miss," said someone from outside and I could recognize the voice.

It was Piyali's voice. And then luckily for me she went to the lateral block to pee.

"This is Piyali." I smiled looking at Trisha.

"Idiot, you are again dreaming." she replied.

I closed the commode and stood up on it and from the space above it peeped into the next block. And with no surprise I was confident she was Piyali.

As she opened her pant and reached her panty I could not resist myself uttering "Hey pink panty, nice legs when do they open?"

Piyali look around as she could not imagine a male voice in a ladies toilet.

"Here up look here." I said.

"You know what one mouse said to the other?" I puzzled her with an idiotic riddle, where as Trisha took hold of my pants to take me aside.

As she looked towards me, Piyali got frightened and started wearing her pants and while it doing, she fall down on her knees hurting herself.

"Mouse said, come to the wall, I will show you my hole" and I laughed running out of the toilet.

Life had never been so funny in the past few years since I had left college. Trisha followed me and we headed towards office.

Piyali too entered the office after first aid on her. I and Trisha kept silent. Piyali knew I was fucking Trisha there, but she didn't throw her anger on me.

In the meeting that week

Piyali sat next to me. The meeting started and we had to give our views to help the bank to grow. Piyali distracted me with a liner on the note *"You like what you saw that day in the public toilet?"*

"Sorry you got hurt with my act." I returned her note.

"There was nothing which you haven't seen; you like what you see?" and the conversation over the note started.

"Yes." A note was exchanged again.

"And you are starved I can see in your eyes; there is no pussy that can keep your dog engaged."

Sittig at one side of the confrence room with my legs being covered by table suddenly she unzipped my trousers and took my dick out. Trish on the chair next to me looked at my tool. She was amazed to see what we were doing under the table.

She coughed intentionally. I took my handkerchief out and put it on the top of my dick and covered it. My ears went red and she continuously stroked me.

"What is winder stroke?" asked Mr. Madhur, it was his lame self made theory.

"When the market goes up and down." he moved his hand on the white board making a graph.

"When it moves up, you enjoy yourself. When it goes down you cry." he said loudly. And at the same time Piyali moved her hand up and down on my dick.

"When it was up you enjoyed yourself."

Piyali stroked it up.

"Now it is down, you have to cry. Results show all."

Piyali stroked it down.

Then the action continued; Piyali moved fast up and down.

"People go by wind, give a blow to the wind, get us the results, and blow it to the banking sector." Piyali was at her full momentum.

"I need the blow, the blow of the wind."

I too blew at the same time Mr. Madhur said blow for the last time.

"Ah." I uttered.

"You have to say something on this blow Mr. Siddharth?"

"Yes no, I mean." I was confused. My dick was out. I was flushed. My ears were red; Trisha was too enjoying it along with Piyali this time.

"What then?" asked Mr. Madhur.

"Nothing." I smiled.

"Okay let's move to the next theory." We knew Mr. Madhur was wasting time.

I was about to zip my pants but suddenly I felt Trisha's hand on my dick. Now she wanted a turn. I looked at her. She pleaded. She knew I owed her a chance. I gave her this chance now. Now I had both Piyali's and Trisha's hand on my dick.

"The theory of two." said Mr. Madhur and it was again a self made theory.

"Let's have an example if we have a client to bond, and he believes in us. Let's lure him to other things too. An account or suggest him to get a card made." He made two balls on the white board. Then he made something like a dick in between. He was way too bad with examples.

"This is what we give." He showed two balls.

"And this is the client." he pointed at the picture of the dick.

"What we have to do is to give him power of two." He laughed and patted his own back.

Trisha threw her pen down, went down the table and sucked my dick taking two seconds, wet it and came up quickly.

"I want each client to have two." Mr. Madhur stressed on the word two while I was too charged to say anything.

With a few more shakes, I came again. My cheeks were red now.

"Are you okay Mr. Siddharth?" I gazed at him zipping my pant slowly.

"Yeah Yeah." I stammered, adjusting myself.

"You don't look okay.?" Mr. Madhur said.

"Yeah actually I am feeling feverish."

I took out my hanky and wiped my face. Then I drank the water kept in a glass.

"Where was I?"

"Power of two." said the two girls simultaneously.

"I think this meeting is over now." Mr. Madhur left the conference room.

The two girls smiled at the sight. I knew it was not a perfect one but this threesome had been better than nothing.

+++ Wise men say: You cannot find the "ONE" if you are still fuckin' with your EX and here I was playing with two fires. +++

After 6 Months, and a time for reward

"Is your fight over now or are there possibilities of a patch up?" Mr. Madhur kept his hand on Piyali's shoulder we all looked at his act in the meeting.

His intentions of touching his female colleagues were always noticeable and we all knew he had a bad reputation. He was our senior so all of us remained quiet.

"It's over sir." I replied.

"So let's move to the important part of this meeting." He asked for the projector to start.

He started his slide which was ill formed and we knew his skills regarding power point presentation. He showed the first slide of the presentation with his name and then he smiled looking at me.

"You know Siddharth, I feel there is something in you and you will grow in life, but your way of hard work is wrong."

"You need a female co- worker to work along with you to get a good start."

"Well that's how the theory of **ying and yang works**." We all knew this was again ome of his self made ridiculous explanations of a therapy.

"Ying for male and yang for females as they come close to each other in their workstations, they can make huge profits." he looked at Piyali to which she nodded.

"So today's meeting is for the reason that our bank is offering a promotion, just one." He repeated the word "just one"twice putting a stress on it. We all knew it would be a female employee who would be getting this promotion. Trisha; one of the hottest babes in the office.

After finishing the presentation which was rather a self portrait presentation of Mr. Madhur he ended the note, "I will look over your overall performance and I will give you a hint for Siddharth being the one who is on the top of the sales."

"I hope all of you will be working hard for the next seven days."

"We need new accounts, more transactions and people opting for bonds and other banking processes offered." He tapped my shoulder before leaving. I could see despair in Piyali's face as everyone appreciated my work.

"Congrats." said Piyali to me before leaving and I opened the door for her.

Before leaving she could not resist saying, "Seven days is a long time, and I find myself in a good position too."

"Better maintain that position, I could see Mr. Madhur's hand on your shoulder. I hope he doesn't have his hand somewhere else."

"You think I have loose morals."

"And Trisha?" she wanted to know.

I didn't say anything for fear of an argument and left for office from the conference hall. I knew this thing had been happening for the last few years. Whenever we fought, we headed for a tough competition and Piyali was good at it.

After entering my office I opened the sales file at once to see my targets. I was just a little below my targets and knew I could manage to get it right on time. Piyali too headed for the central file room to look for my targets and match them with hers.

To achieve my target which was short on two accounts, I called Akash and Jenny for help. But it came to my notice that Piyali had already convinced them to help her. I was screwed and now it was a tough competition for me. I called my home back for the account as I needed to fulfill my targets. I opened two accounts of my relatives so as to save myself and was now happy.

Piyali was also trying hard, I could see her continuously going to Mr. Madhur's cabin with one button opened to distract him. She could throw her pen down or intentionally would bend down to show her cleavage to Mr. Madhur to get a response. I knew Piyali was smart to manage something like this.

The brutal Truth

Apart from the hard work I Piyali and I were doing in the office, I was happy with the way life was going. I had two pussies to play with. But I was still confused about Trisha not for long.

Rings

"Hello." Said Trisha from the other side.

"Yeah Trisha?" I asked.

"Can you help me?" she requested.

"Yeah what happened?" I asked.

"Can you come to a clinic with me? I am expecting my boy friend's baby and he is not helping me out." she said all in a single breath.

"Are you joking?" She reminded me of an incident with Piyali.

"No please help." she pleaded, her voice sounded helpless and soft as if she were weeping from within.

"Where are you right now?" I asked.

"GK2." It was the same place Piyali had suggested jokingly.

"Okay."

Wasting no time, I took an auto rickshaw and accompanied her there. Then we headed for one for the secretive clinics where one could get an appointment with a gynecologist. I had researched for this place for Piyali and now I sat here along with Trisha.

Everything remained silent for the next few minutes, Trisha was feeling guilty and I knew nothing could be done now. So to ease the petition, I broke the silence.

"Whose baby is this?" I asked.

"I am a slut." she replied.

"I don't know how many men have fucked me, how would I know which one?" I could not believe myself. I looked at her; I had a feeling of hatred for her now.

The nurse called us both. As our number came, we went in. It did not take much time to kill the innocent unborn.

It was hard for to me to swallow I was a culprit but that night I could not sleep. Early in the morning as I was trying hard to sleep a message came from Trisha's number: "Thank You Sid, meet me at the office."

In the office I took little time to adjust to my daily routines. Then I went to her desk.

"Piyali is going too much to this bastard's room." Trisha said to me.

"What do I have to do with it?" I said to her in reply looking at Piyali. A smile exchanged between Piyali and Trisha as she went out of his room.

"You should care."

"Why should I?"

"You know what when I was pregnant; carrying a baby, you cared; I can really see a good man in you." she looked different today.

"That was a moral responsibility." I answered.

"You had also slept with me, may be once" I continued.

"And once is enough for me to care." I stared at her.

"And how many times with Piyali?" this was a brutal question just like a wound to be peeled off.

"Forget it." I try to skip.

"So won't you ask me whose baby it was?"

"No." I again avoided.

"It was Mr. Madhur's baby." It was a real brutal confession from her.

I was shocked hearing it as I never thought him to be such an irresponsible person. +++ *As wise men say: Every office has naked truth; you just have to be naked to know it.* +++

Five days and sixth Night

I knew I was now a part of the dirty game. But I wanted Piyali to be out of it. Piyali was going dirty with Mr. Madhur so my loss would gratify her. I quit from the target and finally let Piyali win. She threw a party; I excused myself.

Later that night…

Rings

"Ah…" I could hear someone crying with pain.

"Hello." I said.

"Hmmm," A voice came as a reply from someone unable to express herself but I could make it out to be that of Piyali.

"What Piyali can you say something?" I replied aloud hearing her voice.

"Nothing." she replied as she put down the phone.

I could not get the code but it was some kind of puzzle for me. I try remembering what she said me in the office.

"I will definitely get this Promotion" for which she was very confident. And something was cooking between Mr. Madhur and her. I was not sure but was confident enough because Mr. Madhur had a wrong opinion about her. She could only offer her sex rather than anything else. I called Jenny up to follow up but she had no clue. Trisha's word struck me like a bolt "You should care."

I was confused; I had no option, nowhere to go. I called Trisha up.

"Hello Trisha, I think Piyali is in trouble." I said everything in one breath.

"I don't know where she is. She just said she might be going to Hotel Shelton for the success party, I was invited but I did not attend as you were also not supposed to … your failure was my failure too." Trisha replied.

Oh how could I miss the hotel Shelton the meeting place. But the bastard must have taken the innocent into hotel room. But it was a tough job to search for a single room in a big hotel as hard as to search a pin in the super market.

I looked for the visiting cards on my desk. I got the hotel number and called them.

"Hello" I said as soon as some one picked up the call from the other end.

"How may we help you sir?" asked the desk girl with her memorized lines to enquire.

"Any booking in name of Mr. Madhur?" I asked.

"Nope." she said without looking as I knew they never revealed their client's identity.

"Oh then from the Bank Kokum?" I asked again.

"Sorry sir we can't help you, there are so many rooms?" she replied while putting down the receiver.

I put down the line and click upon an idea. Nothing came into my mind so I called Mr. Madhur's number from the landline in my neighbor's apartment.

"Hello, sir this is Shelton room service, this is just to check the identification via mobile services.

"So you are Mr. Madhur from Kokum bank working as manager?"

"And you occupied room no…"

Before I could complete my statement, Mr. Madhur shouted ***"Room no 321 what a fucking service is this, checking number by calling me on my mobile phone and asking me my identity. I am an old client of yours I always check in to room no 321, I will talk to you manager in the morning."*** He blew upon me as if he was in a hurry and he banged the phone down.

This was enough for me. Then I again called Hotel Shelton.

"Yeah send a bottle of wine to room 321 urgently and do send me your transaction ID so that I can transfer you money online."

"Give me your number I will put money into it."

"Say it's complimentary from Siddharth when you serve."

"Okie Sir once we receive the payment we will revert you back for the note."

I made an internet transaction from my blackberry and with no time the receipt for the complimentary item came as a message from the Hotel's help desk.

I my plan was that the wine would keep Mr. Madhur busy till I reached the hotel rescue the innocent girl. Yes she was innocent here because she was in trouble just because of me. I was the one who had been fighting with her for the last seven years and that was the reason that she was doing something wrong to prove her a winner in this fighting game.

I was on my way in the car. I drove it very fast; the hotel was not very far from my flat and just a 30 minute drive. As I reached the gate of the hotel I threw the keys on the gatekeeper and ran inside skidding on the floor and in a minute wasting no time I reached the help desk.

"Room no 321?" I asked aloud.

"Three floors up." she pointed towards the elevator.

I ran towards it but it was on the way from the ninth floor and three floors were not much to cover with stairs so I took the stairs. My cardio was not that perfect but that day I ran up to my levels. And as I reached the room my heart pounds and I felt like puking. I was afraid. This room and from here the decision I would take would change my entire life. It was a now or never situation. Whether a bad sight or something bad was waiting I had to be prepared.

"Room service." I knocked on the door.

"I don't want anything." Mr. Madhur shouted from inside.

+++*As wise men says: There is only two sources of temptation in this world which can do miracles; Whiskey on the rocks and hot Girl on the bed*+++

"Sir, wine." I asked politely trapping him.

"I said I don't want." he shouted again in anger.

"Open it else." I barked aloud in anger and threw my fist on the door.

He opened the door and he was in his white under wear. His legs were hairy and he was all dipped in sweat. I was like into blood looking at him. I threw a punch on his face with anger; he fell on the floor and hooked up with his injured jaw which was just bleeding with my hard blow.

"What is this Siddharth?" he could not believe this from me. Neither could I believe myself to hit someone so hard.

"Siddharth this may fire you" he was scared.

"And what about the fire that is in my heart now, you raped her bastard." I said loudly kicking the shade lamp nearby and it broke in pieces.

"What if I like a butcher cut you into pieces and pack you here only" I said with full anger.

"You raped that girl." I said again, I could believe myself. I knew I had lost Piyali.

"Who?" Mr. Madhur asked.

"Piyali." I took her name; I took hold of the shade lamp's rod.

"That bitch she called me to this hotel. We were high and then we came to this room. Now she has refused me. When I took off her clothes by force she just slapped me." Mr. Madhur narrated everything just like a small kid.

"And you are alleging me of rape. I took Viagra too." I could not say anything to the old man who was blind in name of lust.

"She is there vomiting in the bathroom," he pointed to one side.

I went inside the bathroom where I found Piyali sitting in one corner with her torn clothes. Her lips were bleeding and her eyes were in terror. As soon as she saw me in the room she hugged me tightly. I took her outside and wrap her with the bed sheet.

"This is how you behave." I showed him her eye which had turned blue with his blow.

"Come." She looked at me very surprreried to see me there helping her at this odd time, helping my life time rival.

"Take this bitch." screamed Mr. Madhur. I kicked him hard on his stomach before I left.

"You both are fired." shouted Mr. Madhur in pain.

"Thank you for the job, my resignation letter will be on your table in the morning sharp at 8 am." I banged the door.

On the way home

"Why Sid?" said Piyali looking at me as I was busy driving.

"What?" I tried being innocent.

"Why did you come to save me?" She asked.

"You called?" I tried to skip this question.

"No; I just did it unconsciously but you came…" Piyali wanted a justification here.

"Why?"

"It is not necessary that I should tell you everything?" I replied.

"Thank you."

"For what?" I asked.

"Nothing." and again we both went into a silent mode.

After an hour's drive and the silence we reached her apartment.Everything stood still.

"You didn't tell why you came to help me?" said Piyali.

"You want to hear why?"

"That's what I wanted to hear." Piyali leaned towards my side.

"You know what we have been fighting for past 7 years."

"Damm, fucking seven years."

"And you know what?"

"What?" she asked.

"I think I am into a habit of fighting with you." It seemed lame but was truly from my heart.

"Loving you may not be that much passionate, people may say its sex which bound us together but I think we are fighting and this is the reason which is keeping us together."

"Together for seven years while fighting and if can fight all these years I think we can fight for a life time."

"I think you must think about it?"

"Think about what?" Piyali opened the car's door and moved out towards the apartment. I wasting no time I also moved behind her.

"Hey stop, at least tell me?"

"Tell what?" Piyali stopped and turned.

"Tell you what Siddharth?" Piyali looked into my eyes.

I could not say anything. My mind froze like my tongue, nothing came into my mind for a fraction of second I thought of hugging her but this was the hardest thing to do at this very moment. She was my girlfriend for so many years. I loved her and respected her, moreover I had fought with her for so long but I had never felt something like this with her and in between us.

"What Siddharth you didn't answer?"

"You know boss took Viagra too." I tried to joke.

"Shut up." said Piyali pressing the button for elevator.

"I wished he would have raped you." I said.

"Do you?" Piyali looked into my eyes.

"No, else I would not have come to help you." I replied smiling.

"Dog."

"You will remain a dog always and forever, and that's what I always say to you." Piyali started moving away again taking stairs this time. I too followed her.

"***Yes I admit I am a dog.***" I finally said breaking the ice and stood there while Piyali kept on climbing stairs.

"***It's just not for me but I admit we, all men are dogs.***" I continued without a pause.

"You know what?" I shouted to attain her attention.

Piyali looked back and I stared into her eyes.

"***Dog is a symbol of faith and I think I will be always faithful to, where ever you need a friend, a lover, a father and a husband.***"

Words started coming out easily from the core of my heart. I knew it and realized it that I loved her but to admit it was a tougher thing. But after today's incident I could see her slipping out of my life, I could not resist myself from saying it finally.

"**To our mother father, wife, daughter, to everyone we are in contact with.**" I increased the inclusion criteria of being a Dog.

"**I love you.**" and everything around us paused for a second. I stared at her lips to read her reply.

+++ *I knew I was a fool because Love was always knocking at my door, but I was always either not at home or asleep.* +++

"Then why you fight with me Sid?" she questioned.

"Because…" I tried to explain.

"We all fight but try to see my heart when I do"

"Ladai to sab karte hain,

Hum ladte to dusre inssan se apni importance leene ke liye,

uski ankhon main unki zindagi khud ko dekhne ke liye."

"We do fight often with the dearest person; we do it not to hurt them but to show them our importance in their life."

C'mon, I really don't know how to propose, I opened my mobile and read the message:

A Mickey without a Minnie,

A Winnie without a pooh

it's just me without you

I quoted dramatically and wait for a reply from her; Piyali came close and hugged me tight. It was the first time the love had overcome lust.

"I don't want to fight any more let's get married, fir sari umar lad lenge." I proposed her finally.

@

{Fucking dog seldom loves: crux the dog who fucks don't marries and one who marries they do what??? Finally Fucks with all the rights, and of course lefts too.}

12

SID WEDS PIYALI

I mailed it to everyone, to new friends and the older one too. Special friends like Jenny and Akash were specially invited along with Mr. Madhur. Our plan was: we were marrying in church and then in a temple for which most of the arrangements were made.

Father started the ceremony with his wedding statements:

Siddharth!

Speak out the name of the bride and repeat along with me: say I love you; I know that this love is from God. Because of this, I want to be your husband so that we might serve Christ together. Through all the uncertainties and trials of the present and future, I promise to be faithful to you and love you. I promise to guide and protect you as Christ does his devotees, as long as we both live. I shall always try, with God's help, to show you the same kind of love, for I know that in His sight we will both be one.

I repeated all of it.

Then the statements shifted to Piyali:

Piyali repeat after me with the name of your would be husband's name, I love you. I prayed that God would lead me to him. I praise him that tonight his wishes will be fulfilled. Through the pressures of the present and uncertainties of the future I promise my faithfulness, to follow you through all of life's experiences as you follow God, that together we may grow in the likeness Christ and our home be praised with his presence.

And Jenny repeated along with the father, while I kept looking at her.

To the final part of the ceremony, Father said: ***Before the two happy couples kiss each other does anyone having a problem or anything?***

Before we could kiss, suddenly the door opened and someone shouted, **"I have a problem father!"**

We looked at Akash who was running towards us.

"You can't marry." he said.

"Why?" we were surprised that what could possibly be the reason Akash had for us not getting married.

"You can't." he repeated.

"You have ruined my life and now you people are marrying."

"Look Jenny you can't marry Apoorv." he shouted at Jenny who was presen there attending our marriage ceremony in the first row.

"*Yahan yeh to dushman bhi shaadi kar rahe hain hum to fir bhi girlfriend boyfriend hain.*" he continued as he looked for Jenny who was completely confused.

"What the fuck are you talking Akash?" Jenny stood up while Apoorv, who was sitting along with her in the ceremony, also stood up.

"Who the hell told you Apoorv and I are going along?" Jenny asked.

Akash looked at me and then pointed towards me.

I smiled "**You know the answer… Okay I accept… I said so**"

"Tell Jenny to marry you, tell her how much you love her." I said giving a chance to Akash.

Akash took a diary from his back pocket and started reading it.

Dear Jenny

"**I love you. Long ago you were just a dream and a prayer but these idiots broke them. This day like a dream come true the Lord himself as he is looking from there, from the sky has answered my prayers that we all can get married in the same church at the same time.**"

"**For today, Jenny, be my joy, be my crown. Thank you for being what you are to me. With our future as bright as the promises, I will care for you, honor and protect you. Would you accept me?**"

"Say yes to me and let's get married."

"Otherwise I will die or kill these two." he looked at me.

"I know you would not like to lose any of us."

"I accept" and a wave of smile ran through the hall. Everyone just giggled, without wasting time Akash and Jenny arranged for the clothes and the ceremony continued with the priest saying:

"Both couples can now kiss and no one will say anything."

"Oh God this generation has gone idiot." He left us behind to kiss. And we kissed till the sun set.

As wise men say: Lovers do wherever and whenever they feel like, oh God! Are you people still thinking about sex; I meant love here."

"Let's quote it again correctly: Lovers express their love whenever and wherever they feel like"

"You are biting me."

"What I never, you always said I am a good kisser." said I pouting my lips and grabbing her butt hard.

"You never had sex or what! It is just a kiss Siddharth don't get desperate." Piyali retreated again.

"C'mon don't fight today at least." I replied kissing her.

"You are fighting." Piyali did not stop because today I was; I mean this dog was chained.

"Then who is fighting? You mean me."

"Yeah shut up and kiss."she threw my body against her, pressing her boobs on my chest.

"You shut up; I am your official husband now." and I continued kissing her.

"What should I do then? I am your wife it doesn't mean you own me." She stopped in the middle of the kiss to ask me.

"Idiot" I smiled.

"Dog." she smiled back.

"Who me?" I asked again.

"If it's not you then who is the dog here?" she laughed.

"C'mon at least take your words back today. It's been years since I have been hearing this." Akash interrupted from the other side.

"Yeah Piyali don't say so." I too joined.

"Not in the church." I continued.

"He is you husband now." Akash tried to defend me too while Jenny stood next to her.

"Hey how can you say so?" said Jenny.

"Husband doesn't mean you have all the wrongs right." She continued.

"Jenny!" Akash tried to calm her down.

"Shut up." she exploded.

"By the way Akash, Can I see that diary of yours where you had been writing all this for me?" he asked.

Akash looked at me "What?" I asked.

"Father took that Diary along with him." Akash giggled.

"Why?" both the girls said at the same time.

"Because it was his vows diary. I just filled in your name." everyone laughed at the Akash's act.

"Is this marriage is confirmed?" Akash asked puzzled.

"Now I agree with Piyali." Jenny said.

"What?" both of us asked confused.

"That, **all men are dogs.**" Both shouted at the same time; I and Akash smiled hugging our loving wives.

EPILOGUE

Do we still need one; well:
**ALL MEN ARE DOGS BECAUSE; DOGS ARE LOYAL,
FAITHFUL AND TAMED…**

Note from the Author

I had plans of writing something serious this time, which you may get to read sometime soon, but then I was told by my fans that they really liked reading my books, which are usually love stories. Not just that, they were keen to know when they were going to get another love story. I had no answer to their questions because I wished to do something different this time. But the problem remained: I had always written love stories only. Then I started writing a few witty lines as and when it came to my mind. It subsequently turned into chapters and now is a full-fledged book.

I'd like to state here that there may be a few incidents in this book which are adult in nature, for which I apologise. Also, the title should not be interpreted in a wrong manner. *It is a humble request to reviewers to not interpret this book as erotica. Lust is also a part of love, if taken as a healthy practice.*

I again want to thank my sweet, lil' ex-girlfriend for the break-up that made me grow up instantly. My world always revolved around her and I could not think of anything else, but now I have a life of my own which I live to the fullest. Special thanks to those who discouraged me with their words, all the way strengthening me and my thoughts.

Emails and feedback from readers will be heartily appreciated.

Note from the Author's Family

Growing up in a closed atmosphere in the valley of Jammu & Kashmir, we never knew Nikhil will take such initiatives in his life. Many a time, he mentioned the book and his writing to us, but we never knew he was so serious about it.

But the day he came up with the e-mail saying he was in contact with a publishing house for the publishing of his first book, we came to know about his serious writing skills.

Our best wishes are always with him.

– From brothers, sisters and all other members of the Mahajan family

Mails from fans for my previous works

Akash Sharma@ hi i read ur "my love never faked" its touching story but in the end it is not very clear that weather priya character is real or fake if it is real then now both of u r together or...

Shibu Kataria@   Hi, Nikhil how are you? hope u r fine,,i m shibu frm delhi.i m reading ur novel my love nve faked...this story is too good...its ur real story... aap ki second book kab tak market me aa rhi hai... plz reply if u hve time. bye.. tke care... shibu

Kunal Patil@ If Ur novel MY LOVE NEVER FAKED is imaginary, then how could be Priya is real character. Is PRIYA a real character? How could u leave her sir? OR she leaves u?

Sanaica malhotra@ hiii nikhil..Sanaica dis side. I read ur novel today....I seriously feel dis was a really beautiful love story... I hate reading novel par I don't know why I chose ur novel 2 read n its really gud one... i dnt hv words 2 express hw beautiful love story it is.. thnks 4 writing such a beautiful love story...

Bhanu Gautam@ Hi! Nikhil i read your book and really I like it most; it is very lovely story and also it is the best story book of my life. Congrats to u for ur writing and I want to know that which is ur next book. About love.....plz tell me...... love u, god bless u................BHANU

Mahi kaur @ I am a huge fan of yours. Last month when I went to the book store, your book" My love never faked" caught my eye and i rushed to buy it. When I sat down to read it I finished it at once. The experience was awesome and chilling. i fell in love with the cute, sweet character of "ABHI" instantly. I was wondering if his character is based on any one you know in real life, probably you? My favorite part of the book was the last chapter where Abhi and Priya unite. I had tears in my eyes seeing Abhi unite with the love of his life. I loved your cool style of writing and I was wondering if you are working on a new novel right now.??

And thanks to Shriya, Wadia, Mohit, Heena,Namrita, Shipra, Alisha, Ruhi,Paras, Mughda, Jagruti, Kiran, Vibha Sharma, Vinay Kumar, sapna, Charu, Payal, Rachna and all my well wishers and fans for mailing me and sorry I could not include each and every email here but would like to thank all those who appreciate my work, love to read it.

Keep reading and keep writing.

Thanks to Deepesh and Vinnie Shetty for their work on FB with their precious updates.

A glimpse into the previous works

My Love Never Faked...: *Author's true story, how he falls for an American girl over Internet. What changed his relationship status from committed to single? And a journey about how he put an end to this stake and got his girl back.*

As Long As I Love You: *A confused love story, a story after a breakup with the crux that breakups are meant for awakening, not sleeping around. A story based on hostel life, parties, friends, and a crush on the teacher.*

A Little Love Incident: *A story on how an email to an author turned into a love story. He was living a life in the limelight and she came to tumble it upside down. Based on real life events.*

"And if you haven't read it yet, you are missing something."

Srishti's all time bestsellers ₹ 100 each

- A Dilli-Mumbai Love Story
- A Feeling Beyond Words
- A half baked love story
- A Little Bit of Love...
- A Little Love Incident
- And then it rained....
- A Roller Coaster Ride!
- As Long as I Love you...
- A thing beyond forever
- Because you Loved me..
- Beep you! you BeepHole
- Boundless Saga of Love
- Can't Cook a Love Story
- Corporate Atyaachaar
- Crazy Bloody Thing LOV
- Everything you Desire
- Few things left unsaid
- Heartbreaks & Dreams!
- I am Broke....! Love me
- I am Still Committed..
- If God went to B-School
- If I Pretend I am Sorry!
- It Happened that Night
- In Course of True Love
- It's all About Love...
- It Should Be u!! My Love

- It wasn't Love at First
- Jab se you have loved me
- Journey of two Hearts
- Life is What you Make it
- Love Happens Like that
- Love, Life & A Beer Can!
- Love, me and Bullshit!
- Love Power Politics!!
- Love a Rather Bad Idea
- LUV is a Dirty Business
- Nothing Lasts Forever
- Of Tattoos and Taboos!
- Oops! 'I' fell in Love!
- Ouch! that 'Hearts'..
- Patyala Down De Throat
- Plz.. Kiss me or Kill me
- She is Single I'm Taken
- 34 Bubblegums and Candies
- That Kiss in the Rain..
- The Idiot-Dudes.....
- The India I Dream of
- The Lost Scraps of Love
- The Off-Site Tamasha
- The Quest for Nothing!
- The Thing Between U & Me
- Those Small Lil Things

- Brain Building for Achievement
- Cheiro's Language of the Hand

- Winning Personality